A Place for Mei Lin

A PLACE FOR MEI LIN

HARLAN HAGUE

FIVE STAR

A part of Gale, Cengage Learning

GALE
CENGAGE Learning®

Farmington Hills, Mich • San Francisco • New York • Waterville, Maine
Meriden, Conn • Mason, Ohio • Chicago

GALE
CENGAGE Learning·

LIBRARY OF CONGRESS CATALOGING-IN-PUBLICATION DATA

Names: Hague, Harlan author.
Title: A place for Mei Lin / Harlan Hague.
Description: First edition. | Waterville, Maine : Five Star, a part of Cengage Learning, 2016.
Identifiers: LCCN 2016024329| ISBN 9781432832742 (hardcover) | ISBN 1432832743 (hardcover) | ISBN 9781432832667 (ebook) | ISBN 1432832662 (ebook) | ISBN 9781432833114 (ebook) | ISBN 1432833111 (ebook)
Subjects: LCSH: Man-woman relationships—Fiction. | Chinese—United States—Fiction. | GSAFD: Western stories
Classification: LCC PS3558.A32343 P53 2016 | DDC 813/.54—dc23
LC record available at https://lccn.loc.gov/2016024329

First Edition. First Printing: November 2016
Find us on Facebook– https://www.facebook.com/FiveStarCengage
Visit our website– http://www.gale.cengage.com/fivestar/
Contact Five Star™ Publishing at FiveStar@cengage.com

Printed in the United States of America
1 2 3 4 5 6 7 20 19 18 17 16

There is no history, only fictions of varying degrees of plausibility.

—Voltaire

CHAPTER 1
WHO DO YOU THINK YOU ARE?

The Rat Trap was the West. It was a place to drink and laugh and tell lies, a place to take your pleasure or drown your sorrows in alcohol or in bed. A substitute for a wife or a refuge from a wife. Or a place to take refuge for a brief moment from the painful memories of a blessed past.

It was distressingly similar to saloons all over the West. Walk in through the front door, and there are half a dozen round tables on the left where at any time of day a few regulars and fewer drifters stare at their cards, trying to read their fortunes. On the right, the long bar that supported two or three patrons, a piano in the center of the room that looked more like a stack of kindling than a musical instrument.

The dark stair at the back, which creaked at each step, led to the four bedrooms upstairs where the sporting women lived and worked.

The rooms upstairs were distressingly similar. An iron-framed bed with a sagging spring mattress, linens as clean as their occupant, a small chest of two drawers, a narrow wardrobe accommodating a dozen hangers that held all the occupant owned. A small round table and single, straight-back chair set before the single window, thin curtains wafting lazily in the whisper of a breeze.

When not occupied at their trade, the women could stand at the balcony rail and look below, each woman wondering who would be her next job, wondering whether, this time, she should kill him or herself, knowing that she would quietly perform her assigned task and dream.

Caleb leaned on the bar, staring into his glass. He swirled the amber liquid and raised the glass slowly to his lips, took a sip, and set it down gently on the countertop, making no sound on the polished surface.

He looked around at a room that was at the same time foreign and familiar. He had never seen more than six or eight men at the tables, drinking and playing cards, never heard the piano played. He rarely strayed from the long bar that was his post and his support.

Caleb Willis was not one that would stand out in a crowd. His handsome face was weathered and lightly creased with lines more common in men older than his thirty-six years. His clothes hung loosely on his trim body, as if they had been bought when he was heavier. They were clean, but faded and a bit frayed at the extremities. His face was shaved, and his light brown hair, halfway to his shoulders, was clean and not very carefully combed. At one time, a lifetime ago, he had cared about his appearance, but that was when he was around people he cared about.

Caleb raised his glass, swirled the liquid and sipped, lowered the glass to the countertop. He glanced down the bar toward the bartender who sat on a tall stool within hailing distance. The bartender wore a soiled light gray shirt, buttoned at the top, always the same shirt unless he had a dozen soiled gray shirts, and a long apron that once was white. He was always there, staring at the opposite wall, looking at nothing. Or deep into his past, for Caleb had not missed the tear that had rolled down his cheek more than once.

Behind the bartender, bottles were arrayed in front of a large mirror that was so clouded at one end that patrons often stood there, laughing at the ethereal image of themselves that showed in the damaged surface. Beside the mirror, there was a print of a naked reclining woman, a hand over her most private part, smiling and fat as a cherub.

Down the bar beyond the bartender, two men stood, each with a boot on the rail, sipping their whiskies, talking softly, occasionally throwing back their heads and laughing loudly. Caleb recognized them. They had nodded to him when he came into the saloon, but he had not responded.

He did not intend to be rude. He had never been considered rude, at least not in his other life. He just did not see any point in befriending people. Not now. He spoke to people when speaking was necessary, and he said only what was necessary. He had not engaged in what might be described as a conversation for at least a year.

A shuffling and muffled voices at the other end of the long bar drew his attention. He turned his head without otherwise changing his position, his eyes adjusting gradually to the dark corner.

Two cowboys were groping an Asian woman. She was young, small, hardly coming to the shoulder of her tormentor. A pretty face, her braided black hair tied up in a swirl on top of her head. She wore a simple cotton dress, a subdued yellow color, longish for saloon wear at mid-shin.

She was pushed against the bar and leaned backward from the weight of the cowboy pressing against her. He rubbed her lower belly with one hand. The other hand was at her throat. His grinning partner squeezed a breast through her dress.

Caleb looked back at his glass, swirled the liquid, raised the glass, and sipped. He recalled the saloons he had known during his wanderings. Most employed women in some capacity. Some tended bar beside the male bartender. Others sang and danced with patrons, all male, men who were starved for female company. They respected these women and treated them kindly.

Saloon owners demanded it.

Then there were the soiled doves, the ladies of the line, the sporting women. They might also mix with the patrons in the saloon, but their function was not to engage in song or polite conversation. Their function was to satisfy the patrons' physical needs in this male frontier. The brothels were upstairs or out back.

The women, whether servers, entertainers, or prostitutes, were often lured to the trade by offers of good pay, exciting work, and nice clothes. Others were widows or poor girls escaping from the drudgery and low pay of mills or farms. Whether they became entertainers or whores depended on their appearance, their employers' needs, and how desperate they were. Most of the women had not chosen their employment. Circumstances seemed to propel them to the life.

"Barkeep," Caleb called. He knew his name, Matt, but never used it. Caleb pointed at his glass. The bartender blinked, pulled abruptly from his reverie. He stood, picked up a bottle behind him, shuffled over, and refilled the glass.

Caleb pulled a coin from his pocket, laid it on the bar top, and pushed it to him. The bartender nodded and picked up the coin. With his other hand, he pulled a handful of coins and a card from his pocket and deposited the pile on the bar top. The barkeep picked a coin from the pile and slid it to Caleb, pulled the remaining coins across the bar top and into his hand cupped at the edge of the top. Dropping the coins into his pocket, he picked up the bottle and returned it to the rack, retreated to his post, sat on his stool, and stared at the wall.

Caleb took a sip from the glass. He picked up the card that the barkeep had left on the bar. It was a picture of a young man with his shirt collar turned up and a stylized letter "D" on the left side of his chest. At the bottom of the card, the words "COBB, DETROIT."

"What's this?" Caleb said to the barkeep.

The barkeep turned slowly toward Caleb and saw the card that he held. "Baseball card," he said. "Comes in cigarette packs. Jack down there drops 'em all over the place." The barkeep pointed toward the far end of the bar.

Caleb dropped the card on the bar and picked up his glass. The barkeep stepped over to Caleb, picked up the card, and tossed it into the trash bin behind the bar.

"Stop! You stop! No do that!" Caleb looked toward the end of the bar. It was the Asian woman. She was not enjoying the attention. She twisted her body and tried to push the cowboys' hands away. She swung at the man in front of her, but he brushed her arm aside. He and his partner laughed.

The saloon madam, also the owner of the Rat Trap due to the propitious death of her husband two years back, stood at the other end of the bar. She was short and chunky, late middle-aged. Her heavy makeup gave her the appearance of a large animated doll. She wore a red dress trimmed with white lace that ended at her knees, but appeared extended by multi-colored petticoats that peeked from under the hem of the skirt. The dress and petticoats were hung with little tassels, sequins, and lace. The low-cut bodice of the dress strained against the weight and bulk of her breasts. Net stockings ended in pointy, heeled shoes. She might have been pretty and stylish once.

She had been watching the commotion at the far end of the bar and had become increasingly agitated. She walked down toward the end of the bar, glancing at Caleb as she passed behind him, to stand behind the cowboys.

"Ease up, boys. You squeeze the fruit too much, you pay the damages."

The cowboy who held the Asian woman looked at the madam over his shoulder and grinned. "Aw, Polly, we're just squeezing a little before buying."

11

"Ease up, Jack, you got no special privileges with my girls."

Jack turned his attention back to the girl, ignoring the madam.

Polly frowned and walked around the cowboys to stand behind the bar. She bent and busied herself with something, or pretended to busy herself with something, looking occasionally toward the woman and her tormentors.

Caleb looked back at his glass, then glanced back at the trio. Jack tightened his grip on the girl's throat. She gagged and made a sucking sound, then a whimper like a tortured kitten.

Caleb swirled the whiskey, raised the glass, and emptied it. He set the glass on the bar deliberately, gently. Straightening, he flexed his back, stepped back, and walked slowly toward the end of the bar. He stopped behind the cowboy called Jack.

"Let her go," Caleb said softly, almost a whisper.

Jack turned slowly. An unlit cigarette dangled from his lips. The opened cigarette pack lay on the bar.

"What did you say? You talking to me?"

"I am," Caleb said softly. "Let her go."

The cowboy straightened and stepped toward Caleb. He still held the girl's throat.

"Now who the hell you think—"

Caleb punched him hard in the stomach. Jack lost his hold on the girl. He doubled over, gasping and eyes bulging. Caleb gripped his arms and helped him back up to a chair and eased him into it. Jack wheezed, rocked back and forth, trying to get his breath.

Caleb turned back toward the bar in time to see Jack's partner coiled for a swing at him. Caleb interrupted the swing with a hard right to the cowboy's head. He crumpled and collapsed, landing hard on the floor. Caleb looked down at him.

Caleb turned and looked at Jack who leaned forward in his chair, his mouth open and glaring at Caleb, his hand at his side. Caleb shook his head, a slow brief movement, a warning. The cowboy moved his hand away from the holster.

The bartender and patrons gaped. They had never seen Caleb in any position except leaning on the bar, never saw him do anything more physical than lift his glass. Five men at a table watched Caleb, their cards forgotten. A middle-aged woman standing behind the table, her hand on a patron's shoulder, looked on in shock.

Caleb looked at the Asian girl who had retreated to the end of the bar. He walked over to her. Her hands were on her cheeks, and tears flowed between her fingers.

She was a mess. Her braid had come loose, and her dress was wrinkled and torn at the neck. Two buttons at the top were undone. A bloodshot eye was encircled with a black ring, and a cheekbone bore an ugly purple bruise. She rubbed her neck.

"You okay?"

"They kill me now." She wiped her eyes with the back of a hand.

Caleb looked for the two cowboys. They stood near the saloon door, glaring at Caleb and the girl.

She looked at them. "They kill me," hardly more than a whisper.

Caleb pondered a long moment, watching the two cowboys, staring at them without seeing them. He turned to look at the wall, distracted, then back at the girl.

"No, they won't." He took her arm and moved her toward the door. She stopped, pulled her arm from Caleb's grasp. Caleb turned back to her.

"I no understand," she said.

He grimaced, impatient. "Do you want to stay here, or do you want to go with me?"

She looked around the room, saw the two cowboys near the door, glaring at Caleb and her.

13

"I go with you." He took her arm again and walked toward the door.

Polly stepped from behind the end of the bar into their path.

"Where do you think you're going!" she said.

Caleb stopped, his hand still holding the girl's arm. On other visits to the Rat Trap, he had seen the woman and was repelled by her. Until now, he had avoided her. Undoubtedly she had noticed his reticence, and they had never spoken.

"Well, ma'am. This little girl isn't safe here. So she's going somewhere she'll be safe."

"She ain't going nowhere. She works for me."

"She just stopped working for you. She can go as she pleases."

"The hell she can. I own her."

Caleb glanced aside, as if he had not heard her, as if he would rather be someplace else. He looked back at the madam. "You don't own anybody. Slavery ended a while back."

"I got a hundred dollars wrapped up in that girl!"

Caleb looked blankly at the madam. He squeezed his eyes shut, looked down. Pondered. *What am I doing here? Am I really involved in this? Does this have anything to do with me?*

He opened his eyes and looked at the madam. He released his hold on the girl and pulled a roll of bills from his pocket. Counting out some bills, he offered them to the madam.

"Here's $50. You'll get the rest soon as I decide no harm's coming her way. We'll be back for her things. If anything's missing, I'll deduct the cost from the $50 coming to you."

The woman did not move. She ignored the proffered bills. "Just who the hell do you think you are, beating up on my customers and stealing my property?"

Caleb laid the bills on the bar. "We'll be back. Have her things ready. All of them."

The madam stood with hands on hips, her face reddening. "By god! You'll pay more than you counted on, mister!"

14

Caleb touched his hat to her. He took the girl's arm and guided her toward the outside door. Near the door, the two cowboys watched. They retreated a step at Caleb's approach. The girl looked at the men and pressed against Caleb. The cowboys watched them walk toward the door.

Caleb glanced at the middle-aged woman who had backed away from the card table and now stood against the far wall. Her frilly dress, cut low in front, identified her as a prostitute, plain and drawn. Caleb had seen her on other visits to the saloon and had acknowledged her. She had always smiled at him, gratefully, it seemed. Now she looked at Caleb and the girl, and a hint of a smile played about her lips.

Caleb and the Asian girl walked through the doorway, and the door closed behind them. The madam glared at the door.

Caleb stepped off the plank sidewalk, still holding the girl's arm. They walked to his horse. He looked back at the saloon door. It was closed. He looked up and down the dusty street. Across the street and down a ways, two old men stood at the hitching rail in front of the general store. They talked with arms and hands, laughing and gesturing. One of them guffawed, bent over, and slapped a knee. There was no one else about.

Caleb turned to the girl. "Climb up behind the saddle," he said.

She looked at the horse, frowned, and looked up at him. "How I do?"

He grimaced. "You never rode a horse."

She shook her head.

Caleb frowned. "Here," he said. They stood on the left side of the horse. He clasped his hands and bent over. "Step in here with your foot, and swing up."

She lifted her right foot and started to step into his clasped hands. He batted the leg aside. "The other foot, the left foot."

She raised her left foot and stepped into the cradled hands. "Hang onto my shoulders, and swing your other leg over the horse." She swung her right leg and kicked the horse's hindquarter, causing him to shy sideways.

Caleb sighed. "God, how difficult can it be to get up on top of a horse," he mumbled. She finally settled behind the saddle. He untied the reins and mounted, with some difficulty since he was not accustomed to human baggage behind his saddle.

"Hold on," he said. She sat with arms dangling. He looked up, exasperated. He reached around, grabbed an arm and pulled it roughly around his waist.

"Hold on!" He almost shouted. She put her other arm around him. Caleb shook the reins, and they moved off at a lope.

CHAPTER 2
MEI LIN

The horse's loping gait caused the girl to move gently against his back. Press and withdraw, press and withdraw, press and withdraw. The movement was strangely disturbing. He leaned forward, but she pressed against him still.

He had left the town fringes behind and now looked at the orange-tinted outline of the Sawtooth range ahead. Earlier than he usually left the saloon. The sun had just disappeared behind the crags, and the filmy cloud layers colored and glowed with its memory.

He frowned. *Now what? The old whore hit the nail on the head. Who do I think I am? I'm nobody. I was somebody once. Had a wife back in Virginia I loved more than life. Two sweet kids that I would die for. But the sickness took them. All of them.*

Nothing was left for me. I wanted to join them in death, but I couldn't even kill myself, though I tried twice. Second time, the doc said my body shut down, and he thought I was gone. When he brought me back, I asked him if I was dead, whether he was St. Peter in his white gown. He told me later that I said that I couldn't see his wings. He laughed when he said it, said I was joking in my delirium. When I told him that I wasn't joking, he sobered and shook his head, patted me on the shoulder.

God, how I wanted to be dead! I hadn't the courage to try again.

Sold my business, told my agent to give the money to poor people, but he was also a friend and would have nothing of it. Said I was not thinking clearly. Said that since I was not working, not looking for work, didn't seem be in a proper mind to do any meaningful work, I would need the money just to live on till I got my affairs and my head settled.

I drifted. In mind and body. Drifted westward, one seedy town after another. I learned to fight. Everybody wants to take advantage of drifters, think they're an easy hit. I got beat up a few times, but I soon could hold my own and didn't mind beating the other guy sense- less and walk away with no regrets.

I bought sex a few times, when I was too drunk to know what was good for me. I always cried, and the whores didn't like that. One actually kicked me off the bed. Another held me and stroked my cheek and cried with me.

Did an odd job from time to time, for something to do. Worked long enough on a couple of ranches to decide that I preferred the company of cows and horses to cowmen and their uppity women. Met some cowboys I liked, good old boys you wouldn't mind spending a cold winter with in the bunkhouse. Others I wouldn't give a bent nickel for.

Drew some cash from my bank account occasionally when I could find a Western Union office, enough for cartridges and a meal. Became pretty good with a six-shooter. Had to use it occasionally on men who wouldn't let me go my own way.

I have killed. Two mean sons of bitches who thought they were bul- letproof. I'm not happy about killing those men, but I don't regret it. They needed killing. Yeah, I know how to use a gun, well enough that when I gather the courage to kill myself, I won't botch it again.

Heard about Idaho. Lonely place, mostly wilderness, small town called Stanley. My daddy's name. Decided maybe I should go there.

He felt the girl's arms tighten around his waist. Her head was on his back and slid gently side-to-side, and her body was on his back, press and withdraw, press and withdraw, with the gait of the horse. She slept.

I got myself into a pickle. What am I going to do with this girl? I can't keep her, and nobody's going to take in somebody that may be a magnet for trouble. Especially a whore and a Chink.

In the gloaming, the trail was barely visible. Here it was a faint parallel double track, a wagon road that was lightly traveled.

They rode over a rising and into his world. He rode slowly now, in no hurry, almost reluctantly, almost home.

Home.

A one-room log cabin, sturdy and tight, a shack nevertheless, but it was all he needed. So he told himself. The wagon was beside the cabin. The two sleek mules in the corral adjacent looked in his direction, like statues, shadows, ears erect. Days, when they were not working, the animals were loose on the meadow. He tried to remember to put them up when going away, but he sometimes forgot or couldn't be bothered.

Beyond the cabin and corral, down a gentle slope, the pond appeared as a dark mirror, reflecting the waning daylight and the rising moon. His claim encompassed four hundred eighty acres of pond, meadow, and woodlands, but he hadn't even seen some of it. Curiosity was not one of his attributes of late.

Caleb pulled up at the cabin. A wave of melancholy swept over him. It was always so, always when he returned home, when he remembered how his wife and his children had been there, at home, how they came out to welcome him, or upon entering, how they looked up and smiled, silently welcoming him.

He shook his head violently and felt the girl jerk upright behind him. She released her hold on his waist, pulling her arms back sharply as if she had touched a hot stove.

He dismounted and tied the reins to the short hitching rail. He wiped his hands on his shirt and reached up to help her down. She extended her arms to rest on his shoulders. He took her by the waist and lifted her from the horse. She felt as light as his saddle.

She fell against him as she touched the ground. Her arms were still on his shoulders, and he felt her breasts press against his chest. He experienced a sudden sensation, a fleeting memory. He withdrew from her and stepped back. She dropped her arms, rubbed her eyes with the back of a hand, and looked around.

He walked to the door and opened it, stepped up through the doorway into the cabin, disappearing into the dark interior.

The girl looked inside and saw nothing. She heard a match strike and saw the flame light the wick on a kerosene lamp. Caleb blew out the match and dropped it into a small bowl on the table.

He motioned for her to come in. She stepped in hesitantly, looked around. The glow from the lantern softly illuminated the interior. Caleb closed the door and dropped the latch.

"Hungry?" he said.

"No. I eat before."

She stood near the door, trying to be invisible. She saw the wooden bedstead against the wall on the left. The edges of two blankets were tucked neatly under the thin mattress. The only other furniture was a small square table with one chair in the center of the room. There was a dark window beyond the table and the shadow of something on the floor under the window.

Against the wall on the right-hand side of the window, there was a sheepherder stove that was both cook stove and space heater. On the facing wall to the right of the stove, there was a counter with shelves underneath and a cupboard. On the wall opposite the stove, a pantry with a door on hinges and an opening to the outside for ventilation and cooling. The outside opening was partially covered with slats to prevent varmints and birds from raiding the contents. All of these units were constructed of hand-hewn planks and nicely finished.

On the counter, one tin plate, a ceramic cup, one knife, and one fork lay in good order, as if ready for service.

"Are you sure?" he said.

"Yes. I like. I hungry."

He glanced back at her, pointed to the chair beside the table. She sat. He went to the pantry where he took out a dish of butter and a slab of ham. From the cupboard, he got a half loaf of bread and cut four thin slices. She watched him spread butter on the bread and cut slices of ham.

"Where you get meat?" she said.

"Farmer on the Stanley road. He keeps pigs." This without looking at her.

"Where you get bread?"

He tapped the stove with his knife.

"You make bread?" she said.

He turned and looked at her. "You're just full of questions, aren't you?"

"Sorry." She sank in her chair and watched him. She straightened. "I help?" she said. He shook his head without looking at her.

He set two thick ceramic plates of sandwiches on the table. She jumped up from the chair and stepped away.

"Sit down," he said. His tone invited no discussion, and she sat. He pulled a small keg from the wall under the window and sat on it.

They ate in silence. For Caleb, it was as it always was. It's time to eat, and so you eat. For the girl, it was a wonderful new experience. She had always had to eat what was left, whenever it was convenient for her owner or her customers, and wherever she could find a place where she could be invisible.

When they had finished, Caleb took the two empty plates to

the counter. He returned to wipe the table carefully with a wet rag.

"I help?" she said.

"You sit." Walking to the cupboard, he rustled around, found a small tin container from a shelf under the counter. He wet a cloth in a pan of water at the cupboard and brought it and the tin container to the table.

He cleaned her face with the cloth, dabbing the bruises slowly and gently. She did not take her eyes off his, though he looked only at her lacerations. When he had finished cleaning the injured areas, he applied a salve from the tin.

"Try not to let this stuff get on the blanket," he said. "It makes a mess."

He walked to the far end of the cabin at the head of the bed, picked up two hides from the floor, a thick buffalo robe and a bearskin, both with the hair on, and arranged them on the floor at the wall opposite the bed. He carefully pulled a blanket off the bed and spread it on the hides.

"Hope you'll be able to sleep," he said.

She walked to the pallet and sat down, pushed gently on the blanket with an open hand, feeling the thickness of the robe, smoothing the blanket. "It best bed I have ever."

He looked at her a long moment, frowned and shook his head, walked to the table, and lowered the flame on the lamp. He sat on the chair and pulled off his boots, tossed them under the bed. Facing the window, away from Mei Lin, he removed his pants and shirt, and draped them on the foot of the bedstead. His gray long johns were a bit frayed at the extremities. Lifting the glass on the lamp, he blew out the flame.

The room was plunged into darkness, but for the soft shaft of light cast by the weak moon through the windowpanes.

He walked to the bed and pulled the blanket down, sat on the bed and looked at the dark outline of the girl, dimly illuminated by the moonlight. She still sat on her bed of skins, watching him.

"Lie down," he said. "Sleep." He swung his legs onto his bed and pulled up the cover with a grunt, rustling and moving about, coming to rest.

She sat on her bed of skins, waiting, until she heard his heavy rhythmic breathing. She lay down slowly, pulled the blanket to her chin, and stared into the darkness.

Caleb stood at the counter, washing last night's dishes in a pan of water on the countertop. He looked over at the stove, checking the progress of the coffee. The water in the percolator had just begun to bubble. He stacked the clean dishes neatly on the countertop to dry.

Carrying the wash water to the open door, he threw it out in a circular spray. He banged the empty tin container on the outside wall, squinting in the bright morning sun.

Turning back inside the cabin, he walked toward the stove. He stopped abruptly when he saw the girl. She was snuggled down in her blanket, and only the top of her head was visible. He had forgotten all about her. *How could I forget her? First time there's ever been a woman here.*

She stirred, turned on her side, and the blanket was pulled from her face. Caleb studied the face. In spite of the bruises, it was a soft face. He had not noticed when he treated her injuries. Yesterday, she had the look of a frightened, injured animal. Now she appeared at peace. *She has a sweet face, a pretty little thing.*

He shook his head, shifted his feet. At the sound, a hand appeared at the blanket edge and pulled it down. She looked up at him, blinking, midway between sleep and waking. Then she saw him, and she remembered what had happened and where she was. She vaulted upright to a sitting position, tensed, hands pushing on the blanket, poised to jump from the bed.

He stepped over quickly and put a hand on her shoulder, pushing gently. "No need to get up. You sleep some more. It's early." *I don't want to deal with you just yet. You stay right there.*

She eased back and lay down, still watching him, pulled the blanket to her chin. She didn't know how to respond, or whether to respond. She was too accustomed to fear what she did not understand or had not experienced.

Caleb walked to the stove counter. She watched his every step, his every move, wide-eyed, wondering, fearful. Caleb picked up the percolator and poured coffee into a cup. He pushed the percolator to the back of the stovetop. She watched, every fiber of her body tensed, ready to leap from the bed and run.

He walked to the pallet and looked down at her. She cringed and held the blanket to her chin. He hesitated, as if looking at a foreign object that he couldn't identify.

"There's coffee, if you want it." He motioned with his head toward the stove, reached over her bed to the wall pegs to fetch a broad-brimmed hat. He put it on as he walked through the door, closing it behind him.

She exhaled, stared at the ceiling. She was suddenly filled with an anxious yearning, hoping that something good was going to happen to her. But did she dare hope? It had been so long.

A shaft of sunlight shone directly on Mei Lin's face. She woke, squinted, and pushed the blanket to her waist. Pushing up on her elbows, she looked around. She was alone. She sat up and leaned against the wall, touched the lacerations on her face and winced. But she felt good, better than she had felt in a long time, a very long time.

She looked at the window and squinted in the sunlight, closed her eyes, and breathed deeply.

She was not afraid. It was the first time she could remember not being afraid. Ever. In her entire life. And she didn't hurt. The lacerations were nothing. She felt good, whole.

She looked around. The walls of the cabin were made of stacked logs, carefully fitted. Thin poles were nailed in the gaps between the logs. A mixture of animal manure and mud further sealed the spaces between the logs.

There was only the single window of glass panes opposite the door. A chest and the small barrel that had served as Caleb's chair were pushed against the wall under the window. On the wall above her bed, Caleb's shirts, pants, hats, and a coat hung from half a dozen pegs.

She had long been accustomed to the chaos and clutter and terror that was her life at the Rat Trap. Here was peace and order.

CHAPTER 3
THEY SOLD YOU FOR MONEY?

Caleb sat on the bank of the small pond. He looked at the strange craft that was tied to the shore with two thick ropes, the bow nudging the bank. A boat of sorts, a barge actually, that rested on pontoons for flotation.

The bare uprights of what appeared to be the beginnings of a cabin, about thirty feet fore and aft and fifteen feet wide, thrust upward. A small pile of lumber was loosely stacked on the shore near the vessel.

He looked beyond the pond down the gentle slope to the valley. The slope was covered in lush two-foot tall bluestem. The waving green blades were just beginning to show the reddish hue of late summer. Scattered about the slope were silver-colored sagebrush and shrubby cinquefoil covered with delicate yellow flowers.

Across the wide basin of grassland and meandering streams, the Sawtooth range thrust upward. Caleb stared at the jagged crags and vowed, as he had vowed many times, to climb them. This view had almost brought him to tears more than once. He would climb the Sawtooths some day and see whether the experience would have more meaning for him than mere exertion.

He looked back at the dredge. The hull was in relatively good condition. He had bought it from a couple of partners who had tried to make a go of dredging for gold on Stanley Creek a few years ago in the late nineties, but they had lacked knowledge, imagination, ambition, and capital, a sure collective deficit that spelled disaster.

Placer gold had been discovered in the creek thirty years before, but it had never been worked extensively due to the hostility of Indians. The Bannocks did not welcome the intruders and made life precarious for them. The Sheepeater Indians were mostly peaceful, but the crafty Bannocks were able to shift the blame for violent encounters on the Sheepeaters.

The most notorious incident was the massacre of a small party of Chinese placer miners. The Sheepeaters were blamed and punished by the whites. It was later found that the Bannocks had killed the Chinese and circulated a false report about a Sheepeater attack.

As the population of miners and ranchers increased in the Stanley Basin, the Indians gradually lost their lands, and game withdrew. The Indians became paupers, living on the edges.

Caleb had no use for the antiquated and abused dredge hardware, and the partners sold it in bits and pieces to hopeful entrepreneurs up and down Stanley Basin. The partners removed the planking of the superstructure to use in building a cabin on a placer claim downstream on the Salmon.

That was fine with Caleb since he decided that he could build a better craft, even though he had no experience with gold dredges or gold dredging. He would take his time and learn as he built.

He occasionally joined the old timers' gossip circle that wasted time sitting around the general store stove, smoking and trading stories and lies. Some had tried their hand at gold dredging and were happy to tell about their experiences. Most of their stories were about why they gave up gold dredging. That was okay with Caleb. At least, they told him what he should not do.

Perhaps he would find two or three men with experience on

dredges to help. But he would not worry if he could find no one. He was not overly interested in success. He wanted only occupation.

He walked to the lumber pile, picked up a plank and dropped it, picked up another, discarded it, picked up another. He shrugged, carried the plank up the board gangway that ran from the shore to the gunwale. He stepped down from the gunwale to the deck and walked over to stand beside the wall of the structure. He stared at the wall, as if studying it. His mind wandered. He saw no wall, no dredge, no prospect.

"What you do?"

He turned to see the girl on the shore near the bow. "Nothing at the moment."

"Why you build cabin on boat?"

Leaning the plank against the wall, he stepped up from the deck to the gunwale. He walked down the gangway and across the grassy bank to the girl.

"It's not a cabin, and it's not a boat."

"I no understand."

He stepped off up the slope toward the cabin. "Let's get some lunch."

They sat in the shade of a tall aspen near the cabin. The small, almost circular leaves shimmered in the light breeze. A few leaves showed a hint of the golden tint of autumn.

They ate sandwiches silently. He watched her. She stared at the Sawtooths. She appeared deep in thought, her mind elsewhere.

"You okay?" he said.

She turned to him. "Okay," she said. She looked down the slope to the valley. Her face betrayed no emotion.

Caleb watched her. *What can she be thinking about? Do I want to know what she's thinking about? Haven't I enough problems of*

28

my own? He looked toward the pond, up at the aspen leaves whipping and twirling in the breeze.

"You okay?" she said.

This girl already knows me.

"What's your name?" he said.

"Mei Lin."

"Your name is 'Leen'?"

"No. Mei Lin. Two word. Mei, like April, May, and Leen,"

"Mei Lin," he said.

"Yes! That good." She smiled.

They ate in silence, looked at the valley and the Sawtooth range beyond.

"What your name?" she said.

"Caleb."

"Cay-leb."

"Caleb."

"Cay-leb." She frowned. "Why you choose hard name?"

"I didn't choose it. My daddy chose it. It was his father's name." He bent over his plate. "Cay-leb's okay."

They looked at each other, an uneasy silence, then turned back to their plates. He stopped eating, watching her as she ate. She glanced at him occasionally, solemn, with a blank face, then returned to eating, head down.

"What are we going to do about you?" he said.

"I help. You need help on boat."

He picked up the sandwich fragment, raised it to his mouth, lowered it to the plate. "Out of the question. . . . Do you have any people here?"

"No."

"How old are you?"

"I not know. Maybe eighteen. Maybe twenty."

"How did you come to be in Stanley? You're the only Oriental here."

"I not Oriental! I Chinese."

He glanced aside, annoyed. "All right, Chinese."

She continued eating, looked up at him, took another bite. "Tell me."

"I shame."

"I don't understand."

"My mother father poor. They say no can feed me. They sell me to man who say he need somebody help him."

Caleb frowned. "They sold you? Just like that? They sold you for money?"

"Yes. Mother father say they love me, but they no want see me die." She looked away, looked at the distant mountains.

"Is that done? Do other parents do this?"

"Many mother father do. They say they do so children can have something eat, so they not die. It called mai zhu zai. It mean 'sell little pigs'."

"I'm sorry," he said. "I had no idea."

They sat in silence, looking at the mountains and the pond and the forest, each waiting for the other.

"How did you get to Idaho?" he said.

"Man who own me, he name Fuhua, he hear about gold in Washington. He come to Seattle on ship, bring me to help. I scare of ocean. I sick most of time. I think I die. I want to die, I so sick.

"We go Rogersburg, place on river. Many people try get gold. We work hard. Very hard. Very hot, very cold."

"How did you come to Idaho?"

"He not find much gold Rogersburg. He hear about gold Idaho. So we go Idaho. Stanley. We find little bit gold. Bad men find out about his gold. They try take from him, and he fight. They kill him. Bad men take me Stanley, sell me madam. That end of story."

"That's all very sad, Mei Lin. I'm sorry. But Mei Lin, it's not the end of your story. It's the beginning. Your life has been filled with sadness. It will be better now. I will help you find a place."

She looked at her hands in her lap. "I no want find place. I here. I want stay here. This my place." She looked up into his eyes. "Please."

"Out of the question!" he snapped. He looked aside. *Why am I edgy? Why can't I just be nice to her? She's fragile. Why can't I be kind?* He lowered his head, stuffed the last wedge of sandwich in his mouth. She looked at him, questioning.

He could say no more. He didn't know how to respond. He could not care for her. He could not provide a home for her. He was an emotional wreck, he knew that, subjected to extended periods of deep depression. He was not often drunk, but when he was, he was neither rational nor gentle. He could harm her and not even be aware that he was harming her. *He . . . he . . . me . . . me. This is not about me! It's about her. This . . . has . . . nothing . . . to do . . . with me. I'm simply not able to handle this. What am I going to do?*

She looked over at him, waited. "You okay?" It was the second time she had asked him the question.

He nodded. "Yeah, okay." He turned to her. "Uh, your owner. Did he ever . . . did you and he ever . . . ?" He paused. *What right have I?*

"Did we sex?"

He nodded.

"Yes, but not lots. He old man. He gentle, almost like he sorry he do."

"You're okay now?"

"Okay now. With you. Men at saloon not good. They hurt me." She put her hands to her face, and the tears came, like a dam bursting. She sobbed.

"Not just body. Hurt me inside, in head, in heart." She

31

sobbed, and her body heaved, shaking, bobbing forward and backward.

Caleb was shaken. This whole affair was outside anything he had experienced. He had no idea how to respond. What would he want if he were in her place?

He moved over beside her. He put his arm around her shoulders and pulled her gently to him. He looked down at her, bewildered. She buried her head in his chest and wiped her face with a hand. She wrung her hands in her lap.

"Please let me stay," she said between sobs, her voice muffled in the folds of his shirt. "Please. I no trouble. I help. I do anything you want. Please."

They looked up suddenly at the sound of hooves on hard ground. Three horsemen rode at a lope down the wagon road toward the cabin.

Mei Lin jerked upright and looked anxiously at Caleb. "Who they? You know? They come get me?"

He frowned, stared at the approaching horsemen. "We'll see." He set his plate aside, stood, and walked toward the riders.

CHAPTER 4
I NOT DO SOMETHING WRONG

The three riders reined up before the cabin. They were roughly dressed, weathered faces, sweat-stained hats, working men. Each mount carried a loaded saddlebag.

"Mr. Willis?" one of the riders said. Caleb nodded.

"I'm Andrew Milner," the rider said. "Steve Adams in Stanley told us you were looking for help and told us where to find you. We're ready to go and would be much obliged for the work."

Caleb relaxed. He liked Andrew already. He was slight, about forty, with a face that showed he had endured hard work and cold winters.

"If Steve sent you," Caleb said, "you're hired. I do indeed need help. I asked Steve to hire men who had experience. You've worked on dredges?"

"Yes, sir. We've all worked on dredges, up north and down near Ketchum," said Andrew.

"Well done. Climb down." The men dismounted. "Glad to have you, Andrew." He shook Caleb's outstretched hand.

"This old rowdy here is Larry," said Andrew, gesturing to the tall, heavily whiskered, broad-shouldered black man. Larry smiled and waited.

"Larry," Caleb said and extended his hand. They shook, and Larry stepped back.

"That sprout there is Johnny," said Andrew, motioning with his head. Johnny lowered his head, avoiding eye contact with Caleb, and shook his outstretched hand.

All three men looked beyond Caleb at Mei Lin. She had followed him from their lunch tree. Now she looked blankly at the strangers.

Johnny, a young man of twenty, had a pleasant face and a tousled mop of blond hair. He had stepped behind the other men after shaking Caleb's hand. When Mei Lin made eye contact with him, he whipped his hat off and held it in both hands. A hint of an embarrassed smile played about his lips. Mei Lin glanced aside.

Caleb ignored Mei Lin and the glances of the men in her direction. He pointed beyond the corral. "There's your bunkhouse. It's pretty rough, but you can improve it any way you like. There's materials on the bank at the dredge, some tools at the dredge and others at the lean-to beside the corral." He pointed.

"There's a good sheepherder stove in the bunkhouse. Hope somebody in your lot can cook. We'll work out provisions. Somebody will drive the wagon to Stanley every week or so for supplies." The men smiled and nodded.

"Sounds good, we'll manage," Andrew said. "I'm a fair cook. Anybody complains has to take my place. That way, there's few complaints." The men laughed.

"You'll need to build a lean-to for your tack," Caleb said. "Use any materials and tools you can find around the place. You can use my corral if you want to, but it's pretty small. You can build your own behind the bunkhouse, if you like."

"Thanks for that, boss, we'll talk about it," Andrew said. "Right now, we're ready to get busy on whatever you have in mind."

"What I have in mind is to finish building this animal," Caleb said, "then find some buckets of gold and make us all rich men. We'll begin tomorrow."

"Whoopee, I'm fer gittin' rich," said Larry. "That's fer sure!"

The others smiled and murmured their agreement. They mounted and set off toward the bunkhouse. Johnny looked back over his shoulder at Mei Lin.

Caleb watched them go, talking, laughing, eager to begin this new enterprise, for that's what it would be for this lot, a new beginning.

What nonsense. For me, at least. I sounded like I was talking to my employees at the plant back in Virginia, encouraging them to work hard, smile and be happy, onward and upward, success is in sight! Well, why not? I don't want to pass on my emptiness to other people, especially people who are dependent on me, people who still think the future has something good for them.

Caleb stood in front of the house, holding a dripping dishpan, watching the horseman riding down the wagon road toward the house. He didn't know him.

The horseman pulled up in front of Caleb and removed his hat. "Mr. Willis?"

"Yep. Get down." The rider dismounted.

"I'm Cal Morse. I heard in town that you was looking to hire men with dredging experience. I worked on dredges down south and sure would appreciate working for you."

Caleb frowned. "Well, I don't know. I just hired three men."

"I work good," Cal said. "I don't need a lot of pay, and I work real hard."

Caleb pondered. "Okay, Cal, let's give it a try. I'll pay you what you're worth." He extended his hand. Cal took the hand and shook vigorously.

"I sure 'preciate it."

"Ride down to the dredge," said Caleb, "and introduce yourself to Andrew. He'll get you set up. I'll be down in a bit."

★ ★ ★ ★ ★

Caleb and Andrew stood on the bank of the pond at the lumber pile. Caleb sorted through the pile, picked up a board and examined it, dropped it and picked up another.

"Did you get Cal situated?" said Caleb.

"Yeah, I had a good talk with him. You know, I knew I'd seen him somewhere, and then I remembered. He was at th' Trap when I was talking to Mr. Adams. He was real interested in our conversation. I wasn't surprised when he showed up today. He ain't the sharpest knife in the drawer, boss, but I think he'll do for a hand."

"Let's give him a chance."

The roof beams of the dredge housing were up, and the siding was almost finished. Sawing and hammering from inside the structure were evidence of progress on the housing.

Mei Lin held a plank in place on the outside wall while Caleb drove nails into it. That done, she selected another plank from the loose stack on the deck. She held it up to the wall next to the plank just attached. The edge was not straight and left an empty slot between the two planks.

"Aí yǎ, bù xíng," she said. She tossed the plank to the deck and picked up another. She held it up for inspection. She frowned and ran her finger along the edge. She held it up against the attached plank. The join was straight and tight.

"Haǒ lē," she said. "Xíng lē." She held the plank in place and turned to Caleb. "Kě yí lē," she said.

Caleb had watched all this. He smiled. "Not bad," he said. "Couldn't have done better myself. But, Mei Lin, I can't understand a word you say."

"What? Oh, I forget. You no speak Chinese." He raised his hammer in mock anger. She laughed and jumped back.

Caleb smiled. She held the plank in place, waiting. When he

simply stared, she cocked her head.

"Are you happy?" he said.

She sobered, frowned, serious. "What mean 'happy'?"

Caleb sighed heavily. "Mei Lin, Mei Lin."

"What? Never mind," she said. "You work. I go cabin make tea."

"Tea," he said. "How about coffee?" She frowned, put on a hard face. "Okay," he said, "tea."

Caleb and Mei Lin sat on a pile of planks on the bank near the gangway. They held ceramic mugs of tea. A metal tray holding a ceramic teapot lay on a plank beside Mei Lin. Caleb sipped his tea.

"Not bad. Not bad at all. I could get used to this. Had a hard time finding it. The Stanley clerk thought I was some kind of pervert, asking for tea. He said he would have to get it from the Chinese up north."

Mei Lin cocked her head. "What mean 'pervert'?"

Caleb frowned. "Um . . . somebody different. Somebody . . . never mind." He downed the last of his tea. He held out his cup to Mei Lin. "Any more in there?"

She smiled, picked up the pot, and poured into his mug, then her own. They sipped their tea in silence.

"Cay-leb?"

He looked up at her. "Yeah."

"Cay-leb, you have old clothes I can wear?"

He had taken no notice that she still wore the thin yellow dress that she had worn the day he took her from the Rat Trap. She had since worn an old jacket of his on cool days, but she owned nothing but the saloon dress.

"I think so," he said. "We'll have a look this evening."

"Thank you. I no like this dress. It remind me too much."

Caleb drained the last of his tea and handed the cup to Mei

Lin. "To work." He stood, stretched, and headed for the dredge gangway. Mei Lin put their cups on the tray, stood, and walked up the slope toward the cabin.

She stopped on the path. A fresh breeze brought the sounds of sawing and chopping from the meadow where there was a long stack of logs. The logs were about four feet long and five or six inches in diameter. They would be cut later into shorter lengths to feed the firebox of the dredge steam engine. As soon as the dredge had a steam engine.

Caleb had hired a couple of drifters to cut the logs and stack them. They had a shifty look about them, and he restricted their access to the forest fringe where they cut the logs, the log pile where they trimmed and stacked the logs, and the bunkhouse.

Mei Lin strolled in the meadow, idly pulling at seeds from the tall ricegrass, stopping to admire a particularly brilliant purple coneflower. She walked on and stopped at the long row of logs. At the sound of sawing on the other side of the logs, she walked around the pile.

Rounding the stack, she watched the woodcutter toss a log on the top of the six-foot high pile. He looked up at her, straightened, and flexed his back.

"That look like hard work," she said.

The cutter wiped his face with a hand. His long hair dripped with sweat. His worn, wrinkled clothes seemed to be hung on his body rather than worn. He looked to be about thirty, but he might have been ten years younger.

"Yeah, it's hard work." He looked her over, grinned. She frowned, pushed a lock of hair from her forehead.

The cutter stared at her, still grinning. "Don't you remember me? I sure remember you."

She frowned again, glared at him. She tensed, stepped back. "Now I 'member. You come Rat Trap. You smell. Same now."

He grinned. "Yeah, I guess I smell like a man. But I think you enjoyed it."

She frowned and turned to leave. He dropped the saw and reached for her. He grabbed her arm and pushed her roughly against the stack of logs.

She struggled. "Stop that! Fàng kāi wǒ, asshole!" she shouted. She swung and struck him a hard blow to the side of his head. He winced. She swung again. He jerked his head backward to avoid the blow.

He laughed and tightened his hold around her shoulders while his other hand ripped her dress open and found her breasts. She tried to pull away, and his arm slipped up tightly around her neck.

She gagged, brought a knee up hard into his groin.

"Umph," he recoiled. He tightened his hold around her neck. "You bitch. I'll break your—"

The cutter was thrown violently sideways by a blow to the side of his head. Mei Lin pulled free and jumped away. Johnny threw the short limb aside. He grabbed the staggering man, whirled him around, and plunged his fist into his belly, a blow that lifted him off the ground. The cutter crumpled to the ground and lay still.

Johnny bent over him, gasping, his face contorted and his legs spread, a coiled spring. Mei Lin cowered and stepped backward against the stacked wood.

Johnny straightened and jerked around to face her. He gasped, charged with the violence of the confrontation, but his face was soft.

"Are you okay?"

"Okay," she said, hardly audible. "Thank you."

"I'll take it from here." Mei Lin and Johnny whirled around and saw Caleb striding toward them. He had watched the incident from the beginning, running from the cabin upon hearing Mei Lin's first cry. Johnny was on the dredge, closer to the woodpile, and reached her first.

"Go on," Caleb motioned with his head toward the dredge, "I need to take care of this trash." He grasped the man by the collar and dragged him toward the bunkhouse, wondering whether he was unconscious or dead. He didn't care either way.

Mei Lin and Johnny walked slowly down the slope toward the pond. As she walked, she fumbled with her dress, all the while watching Caleb over her shoulder, striding up the slope with his inert burden. She almost stumbled as she watched Caleb disappear around the pile of logs.

Johnny looked straight ahead, only glancing occasionally at Mei Lin, looking back sharply to the front as she tried to repair the damage to her clothing. When she stopped at the embankment near the dredge, Johnny quickened his pace without a word and walked up the catwalk to the dredge deck. He disappeared inside the housing.

Caleb released the man, or the body, in front of the bunkhouse. He walked into the cabin and reappeared a moment later, dropped a canvas bag and an armful of clothes on top of the man. Staring at the debris a moment, he shook his head and walked down the slope toward the dredge.

Caleb saw Mei Lin who sat on the embankment beside the dredge, looking down at the valley. He stopped beside her, and she looked up. They exchanged a long silent look.

Mei Lin winced at Caleb's severe face. He turned away and walked toward the dredge.

"I not do something wrong," she called after him. He did not look back.

Mei Lin awoke early the next morning in her bed of skins and blanket. She watched Caleb pour coffee and walk silently through the door, carrying his cup. He did not look her way.

The door closed behind him.

And so it was for the day. He hardly noticed her. It was as if she weren't there. He prepared his own lunch. He ignored the tea she made in the afternoon and did not invite her to help on the barge. He ate his supper standing at the counter rather than at his usual place at the table.

Sitting in her chair, she looked up at him. Tears welled up in her eyes. "I not do something wrong."

He turned his back on her to wash his dishes.

Mei Lin woke the next morning at first light. Caleb, fully dressed, stood over her, waiting for her to wake up. He held a small packed saddlebag. She sat up and looked up at him. And waited.

"I'm going away a couple of days."

"Where you go? Why you go?"

"Stick close to the house. I told the men."

"Cay-leb?"

He shouldered the saddlebag and walked through the door. The door closed, and the latch dropped. Tears streamed down her cheeks.

Why? Why? Why? Why do I torment that girl? Why can't I be good to her? I don't want to hurt her. What do I want? Why am I holding back? I want what is best for her. Why do I think I know what is best for her? I'm going to come to no good end, I know that, and I don't want to pull her along with me. She has no future with me. She says she wants to stay with me. Of course, she does. She was a whore in a dangerous situation, every day a trial, death always a possibility. But am I her salvation? Me? I can hardly cope. How can I help her?

He rode on a game trail through a meadow of short buffalo grass. The long blue-gray blades showed a slight reddish hue, signaling the approach of autumn. Scattered maples along the narrow, meandering stream showed a hint of color. Hillsides on each side of the valley were dotted with dark pines and juniper.

Night. Caleb sat at a small fire, his saddle and blanket beside him. His hobbled horse nibbled grass at the edge of the firelight. Huge dark cottonwoods loomed over the site, the heavily leafed lower branches lightly illuminated by the fire, creating the illusion of a dwelling interior.

He stared into the flames.

Mei Lin sat under the shade tree where she and Caleb often sat together, eating lunch or simply enjoying the view of the meadow and mountains. Tear tracks marked her face. She closed her eyes and wiped her cheek with a hand. She rocked back and forth, trying to hold back the tears.

She wore the pants and shirt that Caleb had given her. She had cut six inches off the pant legs and stitched a hem in them and narrowed the girth of the shirt with a vertical cut in the back, then stitched up the two sides. The sleeves were rolled up to her elbows.

"Miss?" Mei Lin jumped, and her eyes opened wide. There stood Johnny with his hat in his hand. She remembered that he had taken off his hat to her that first day.

"I don't mean to bother you, miss, but I know the boss has been away these two days, and I saw you up here, and I wondered . . . uh, I wondered if there is anything I can do for you. Sorry to bother you."

She relaxed. "You no bother me." They looked at each other. He wrung his hat and looked aside in both directions. He looked down the slope to the dredge and back at her.

"You want sit down?" she said.

He fidgeted and looked back at the dredge. He turned back and sat down slowly in the shade of the tree five feet from her.

He held his hat in his lap. They looked at each other and at the mountains and the meadow and the dredge.

"What your name?" she said. "I forgot."

He jumped at her voice. "Johnny, ma'am."

She smiled thinly. "I not ma'm, Johnny, I Mei Lin."

"Hi, Mei Lin." He smiled. They looked at the valley and the mountain, glancing back at each other, smiling. A single bead of sweat rolled down his temple.

"Thank you, Johnny."

Johnny blushed a deep crimson. "It wasn't nothin'. You did right in yelling loud. I'm sorry you had to watch. I just lose my head when I see somebody hurting a horse or a dog or . . . oh, I don't mean—"

Mei Lin smiled. "I know what you mean, Johnny. You good man."

Johnny squirmed. He jumped up. "Well, I guess I'd best be gettin' back to work." He started to go, then turned back. "Uh, miss, uh, Mei Lin, if there's anything I can do for you, please give me a holler, and I'll come runnin'. Please do that." He turned and ran down the slope to the dredge.

Mei Lin watched him go. She lowered her head and wiped her moist eyes with the back of her hand.

The sun was low on the western horizon when Caleb rode into Stow. Or what was left of Stow. The Englishman who had founded the town, perhaps homesick, had named it Stow-in-the-Valley, but the name had never caught on. A typical comment from newcomers was a variation of: "Stow-in-the-Valley? What the hell kinda name is that?" The name survived simply as Stow.

The town had been a thriving community of six hundred souls when the mine was flourishing, but declined when the mine played out. Now only twenty or so families called it home.

Caleb rode slowly down the single street, his horse's hooves raising little puffs of dust. A one-room schoolhouse on the left was shuttered, the white paint peeling on its sides. Beside the schoolhouse, the picket fence of a cemetery of two dozen graves sagged, some pickets loose and leaning, some missing.

On the right side of the road, a blacksmith in a soiled apron stood before his small shop that was set back from the road. He wiped his hands on his apron and watched Caleb. His stern look said what th' hell you doing here?

On each side of the smithy, buildings that once had been thriving shops of some sort now sagged, doors off their hinges, shingles missing, windows with broken glass panes, paint peeling, exposed decaying timbers.

On the slope behind the row of ruined buildings, the rusty bones of the mill thrust upward from the shroud of dark pines.

Caleb was seized with a deep melancholy. He shook his head and swallowed, choking back the tears. He rode on.

On each side of the street, thin smoke spirals from chimneys of small ramshackle houses told of the precarious existence of their occupants. A woman dressed in a shapeless faded cotton dress stood on a front porch, leaning against a post, her arms folded, watching Caleb. Small gardens were laid out in front or beside some of the houses. No one worked the gardens.

Past the ghost of Stow, at the far edge, Caleb rode into a thriving community. The Chinese who had served the miners had stayed after the mine failed and the mining community had disappeared. As long as the mine flourished, the Chinese had washed the clothes of the miners and shopkeepers. They had cooked and cleaned for them, and they grew vegetables for them. Now they cooked, cleaned, and grew vegetables for themselves. They were not prosperous, but they were self-sufficient, and they were content.

Small neat houses lined the road, widely spaced with vegetable gardens in front and alongside. In some of the gardens, a man or a woman worked, clearing weeds or bending to gather vegetables. Two women walked on the road, chatting loudly, laughing.

Caleb reined in at a large garden fenced with short pickets where two men stood between rows of potato plants. They had stopped working when they saw him riding up and now watched him intently. Each man held a digging fork. Freshly unearthed potatoes lay loose on the ground before them, two partially filled buckets in grooves between the rows.

Caleb dismounted, tied the reins to the fence, and walked through the open gate. "Neat garden you've got here," he said. The men nodded. They had not taken their eyes off Caleb and held the forks with both hands.

"Bit late for potatoes, isn't it?" The men relaxed. They smiled and lowered the forks.

"These late potatoes," one said. "We dig some in summer, some now. These late. We like potatoes. You know potatoes?"

"Used to grow some back east. Virginia," Caleb said.

The man sucked in his breath. "Ooh, that long way. I don't know 'bout Virginia. Idaho grow good potatoes. Better than my home China."

The other man stepped up and bowed slightly. "You want tea? Time for tea."

"That would be very nice. Thank you, I would. I like tea. A friend introduced me to tea recently, and I like it."

The man nodded and walked to the small house behind the garden, disappearing inside. The other man motioned toward an arbor and walked to it. Caleb followed him.

Under the arbor, Caleb looked up. The vine that covered the arbor was losing its leaves. Some of the tendrils were bare. Others held dry, crispy tan leaves and some that showed the subdued colors of early autumn. The man motioned toward the chairs at a table, and they sat down.

45

The man who had gone into the house returned with a tray bearing a ceramic teapot and four ceramic cups. He set the tray on the table, nodded, and walked through the garden gate to the road. He closed the gate and walked briskly down the road.

The man who sat with Caleb poured tea, and they sipped silently. Presently the other man who had made the tea returned with another Chinese. The man sitting with Caleb rose and bowed to the newcomer. Caleb also rose. The newcomer nodded and motioned for all to sit. They sat, and tea was poured for the two men.

CHAPTER 5
I NEVER HAVE PRESENT

The sun had just dropped behind the Sawtooth range, and the cloudless sky at the horizon was a brilliant orange-yellow, blending upward to a light turquoise.

Caleb walked his horse down the wagon road toward the house. The mules in the pasture stood like statues, ears erect, watching him come. One of the mules sounded off, a whinny that became a bray and ended in what sounded like a rolling belly laugh.

The cabin door burst open, and Mei Lin ran from the cabin into the yard. She had long ago associated the mule's greeting with Caleb. Holding a stout piece of stove wood at her side, she watched him come.

Caleb pulled up before the hitching rail. He looked at Mei Lin who looked back at him, sternly, without blinking. Dismounting, he tied the reins to the rail and turned to Mei Lin.

"I hope everything—"

"No nothing talk! You tell me where you go! Why you go! Now! You tell me!" She waved the stove wood in his face.

Caleb retreated a step. He wanted to smile, laugh, maybe grab her. "Okay. Let's get some supper. I'll tell you everything."

They sat at the table, Mei Lin in her chair and Caleb on the keg. Caleb's plate was empty. Mei Lin's had not been touched. Her hands were in her lap. She glared at him.

47

"They said they would be glad to welcome you. You would have to work, but you would be safe. They said that nobody bothers them. They get along well with the Americans who still live there, and that attitude seems to insulate them from outsiders."

"No! I happy here." She did not smile. Her look was one of resolution, neither submission nor timidity.

"It would be best for you. It's going to get nasty here. The sentiment against Chinese seems to be growing. Mei Lin, up north they have a tree they call the Chinese Hanging Tree. And they tell me in Stanley that the owner of the large dredge off the Salmon is raising hell with the owners of small dredges. He wants no competition. There could be trouble."

"No. I not go. I not afraid."

"You may not have a choice."

"I kill myself," she said.

He softened. "Don't talk like that."

"I kill myself!" She looked at Caleb as tears streamed down her cheeks. "I happy here," she said softly. "It first time ever I happy."

Caleb turned and looked at the dark window. "Mei Lin. Mei Lin."

The days passed, and there was no more talk of Stow. Caleb and his four workers finished the dredge housing, and Caleb sent word to the railhead office in Ketchum to inquire about the delivery of the dredge buckets, cylinder, steam engine, and other hardware.

The reply from Ketchum was encouraging. The delivery was on schedule. The shipment should arrive there in two weeks. It was getting late in the year to begin dredge operations, but Caleb was anxious to get in a few weeks of work before winter closed them down.

Mei Lin had watched Caleb as he carried out his usual household chores, and she gradually took over. She now did most of the cleaning and had taken to washing his clothes, though he had protested at first. Just do your own things, he had said, and I'll do mine. She had ignored him, and soon he was content to drop his dirty clothes on the floor and find them washed, dried, and hung on the wall pegs the following day before supper.

She washed her own clothes at the same time. Caleb had been surprised on his return from Stow to see her wearing the old clothes that he had given her, which she had altered. He had wanted to say something, but it didn't seem the right time. When they had reconciled and Stow had been put behind them, Caleb had commented and said that she looked like a clown.

"What mean 'clown?' she had said. When he explained the meaning, she replied that she didn't care. She was glad to burn the saloon dress.

She also had watched his cooking and meal preparation and soon was doing most of the cooking and all of the cleanup after meals. He often stood in the center of the cabin, watching her. He had difficulty knowing what to do with his hands when he normally would have been cooking or cleaning up and putting away.

Her first attempt at baking bread was not successful. She had watched Caleb making bread, and she had welcomed his instruction at first, but when she interrupted him repeatedly with her "I can do!" he backed off.

Her first loaf looked like a large, fat, beige slug. Even the birds rejected it. Next time she made bread, she asked for help and was more attentive. Since then, she had become expert and had received high praise from the bunkhouse as well as Caleb's nod. He never made bread again.

A casual visitor would have concluded that Caleb and Mei

Lin were husband and wife. But they were not, for there was no intimacy. They had hardly touched each other, just a brush or casual touching when passing a plate or tool. Each welcomed the other's company, sharing space and chores, but each withheld sharing their souls for their separate reasons.

Yet each occasionally watched the other when the watching could be done without notice. Questioning, wondering.

On a sunny afternoon, Caleb walked on the path from the cabin down the slope toward the dredge. He stopped. Mei Lin and Johnny stood together on the deck. She held a board up to the wall, and they cooperated in lining it up. Caleb heard their laughter.

He pondered. *Is Johnny the solution for Mei Lin? He is her age. He has proven that he cares for her and can protect her. He is a good worker and will make his way in this god-cursed world. He could make a place for Mei Lin.*

He watched them. Mei Lin held the board against the facing. Johnny positioned the nail on the board, raised the hammer, and struck the nail. After striking his thumb. He shouted and dropped the hammer that clattered on the deck. He shook his hand and sucked on a finger.

Mei Lin doubled over laughing. She took his hand and rubbed it. She giggled while Johnny stared at her, mesmerized. Caleb could almost feel his stare.

Yeah, Johnny. She can be distracting.

Caleb turned and strode back to the cabin, his head full.

The cabin interior was darkening with the waning day. A shaft of sunlight from the window described a patch of light on the floor. Caleb worked on the cabin wall, troweling daubing from a bucket to the spaces between the logs. Mei Lin sat at the table, watching him. Her elbows were on the table, and she rested her chin on her hands.

She pulled the lamp to her, struck a match, and lit it. Caleb looked around at the sudden brightness, then turned back to his work.

"Cay-leb." He ignored her.

"Cay-leb, you not speak for hours. You okay?"

He glanced over his shoulder at her. "Of course, I'm okay. It's all right if I work on the walls, isn't it?" She winced, and he noticed.

"Sorry, I'm just a little . . . out of sorts," he said.

She frowned. "What mean 'out of sorts'?"

He dropped his hands to his sides and stared at the wall. "Nothing. Let's get some supper."

He walked to the door, opened it, and set the daubing bucket outside on the ground. Standing in the doorway, he stared at the woods across the road, his mind racing.

He walked to the cabinets. Mei Lin closed the door, walked over to stand beside him. They made their meal together, silently, Mei Lin glancing at him while he studied the potatoes, squash, onions, and elk roast.

They sat at the table, Mei Lin in her chair and Caleb on his stool. Their plates were empty. The lantern on the countertop made a soft light on their faces. Mei Lin watched him and waited.

The meal was finished. He had to either get up or talk. He stared at his plate, picked up his fork absentmindedly, replaced it on the plate.

"Did you and Johnny get the wall finished this afternoon?" he said.

"No. He hit his hand and hurt it."

He looked at her. "Yeah, and you laughed at him. Don't get

in his way, Mei Lin. He's a good worker, and you're distracting him."

"But I just try . . ." She stopped. Her eyes opened wide.

"That it! That it! You jealous!"

"Jealous? Nonsense!"

"You jealous! You jealous!" She jumped up and ran around the table to him. He stood quickly to fend her off. She grabbed his shirtfront, pulled his head down, and kissed him hard. She pulled back and released him, her hands on her cheeks, startled at what she had done.

He smiled thinly, pulled her hands from her cheeks, and held her hands. He leaned down and kissed her softly on her lips. He put his arms around her shoulders and pulled her to him, resting his head on hers, his face buried in her hair, breathing in her perfume.

"Mei Lin, Mei Lin," he said softly. "What am I going to do about you? I can't keep you. It's not fair to you. What are we going to do?"

Mei Lin held him tightly, her head pressed against his chest, and said nothing.

Mei Lin continued to help on the dredge, but as the construction neared completion, she had more time to simply enjoy her cloistered existence. Sometimes when her chores were finished, she sat alone under the tree where she and Caleb usually ate their lunch, staring for hours at the magnificent Sawtooths.

One pleasantly cool day, she strolled in the pasture, sweeping the grass tops with her hand, pulling seeds and chewing on them.

She stopped her walk in the meadow when she saw Caleb's horse ahead. The horse pricked up his ears and watched her. The horse was a buckskin gelding, the color of tanned deerskin, about sixteen hands. Sleek and muscled, with a dark mane and tail and lower legs, almost black.

She walked over to the horse and touched his muzzle. The horse raised his head, and she stroked his cheek. She talked softly to him, pulled at his mane, and rubbed his back and sides, talking all the while.

When she walked slowly away, the horse followed her. She stopped, stroked his back, walked again, looked back to see him following again.

Caleb stood on the bank near the dredge and watched all this.

That same evening, Caleb stood outside the cabin, drying his hands on a dishcloth, and watched Mei Lin in the corral. She stroked his horse's back and rubbed his muzzle, talking softly to him. She walked slowly away and turned to watch him follow her. She stopped and stepped over beside him, stroking him gently.

Mei Lin rubbed the horse's back with both hands. Then she dropped her hands to her side and took a deep breath. Facing the horse, she shuffled on her feet and braced herself.

"Uh oh," Caleb said softly to himself.

Mei Lin took another deep breath, grasped a handful of mane and swung herself up on the horse's back. The horse instantly shied, bucked, and she slid off, falling heavily to the ground on her stomach. The horse walked to her and nudged her shoulder with his muzzle.

She stood and flexed her back, hands on her hips. She put an arm over the horse's neck and spoke softly to him. She stroked his back, grasped a handful of mane, and swung up on his back. The horse immediately bucked, spun, and she slid off, landing hard on her butt, rolled, and came to rest on her stomach.

She lay still a moment, then pushed up on her elbows. The horse walked to her and nudged her in the back.

She stood slowly, painfully it seemed, and grabbed a handful of mane. She shook a finger in the horse's face, talking softly to him. She walked toward the corral gate, rubbing her butt. The horse followed.

Caleb walked to the corral. He opened the gate, and she walked through. He closed the gate behind her. The horse walked over to Caleb. He reached over the corral pole to rub an ear. Mei Lin rubbed the other ear.

"Your horse not like me," she said.

"He's pretty particular."

"Your horse have name?" said Mei Lin. "You never say."

"Buck," he said.

"Why Buck?"

"Well, partly for his color, buckskin, and partly for the man I got him from. His name was 'Buck.' A stupid man who lost his poke at cards and finally bet the only thing of value he had left in the world. His horse."

"Pretty dumb," she said.

"Yeah. I paid him anyway. From the money I had just won from him."

"You good man."

Caleb shook his head, smiled.

Caleb sat on the wagon seat, holding the lines of the team. He swayed back and forth as the wagon rolled down the road toward the cabin. He pushed lightly on the brake with his foot to slow the wagon on the descent.

He had told Mei Lin when he left that morning that he had business in Stanley and that he had to buy supplies. Yeah, he had lied, but now he smiled at the subterfuge. Behind the wagon, a pretty little mare was tied.

The very moment he saw the mare in the sale corral behind the livery, he knew this was Mei Lin's horse. She was sleek and muscled, about fifteen hands, three or four years old, a smoky gray color. She had a pretty neck and head, and her tail and mane were long and coal black. There was a distinctive black stripe down the middle of her back. He paid more than he should have, probably less than she was worth, and he was pleased.

Caleb's horse in the pasture nickered a greeting, and Mei Lin appeared in the cabin doorway. She saw the wagon approaching and walked toward it.

Caleb pulled the wagon up in front of the cabin. He wrapped the lines around the brake handle and jumped down. Mei Lin stared at the mare. Caleb followed her stare.

"I found her on the road. Pretty thing, isn't she? Friendly, too. Guess she's lost."

Mei Lin walked to the mare. She ran her hand lightly down the horse's back. The mare nipped at her hair. Mei Lin smiled.

"You pretty girl," she whispered. "You lost? Where you live?" She turned to Caleb. "Poor girl. I wonder who own her."

Caleb smiled. "You do."

Mei Lin frowned. She looked at the horse, then at Caleb. "What you mean?"

"I mean that she belongs to you. A present. She's your horse."

Mei Lin stepped back awkwardly. She held her cheeks in her hands, then covered her entire face. Tears flowed through her fingers. She lunged for Caleb. She fell against him, forcing him to step back to regain his balance. She reached around his waist and held him tightly, her head pressed into his chest.

She leaned back and looked into his eyes. She took his cheeks in her hands and pulled him down. She kissed him softly, pulled back, and patted his cheeks lightly with both hands, then again, this time almost a slap. Caleb winced, smiled, and glanced aside.

She bent over with her hands between her knees, straightened, tears marking her cheeks. "Cay-leb. I never have present." She ran around the wagon to the horse. She stopped beside the mare, looking her over, her hands on her cheeks.

"I can't believe." She turned to Caleb. "She really mine?"

"Yes."

Only then did she see the saddle in the wagon. She looked at Caleb. "That too?"

"Yes, that too."

She dropped to her knees, her head lowered and her hands folded on her chest.

Caleb walked to her. He looked down. "Are you okay?"

She spoke softly without looking up. "I so happy, I think I die."

"Don't do that," he said. "This little mare would miss you." He pulled her up. "She'll want to get to know you as much as you want to get to know her. She'll smell your hair, your shoulders, and around your neck. Fellow in the sale barn said to let her smell your hand. Don't know about that. She might think you're offering her a treat. Let her smell the back of your hand. Soon as you two feel comfortable around each other, untie the reins and lead her into the corral. Tell her that she's a lucky girl to have a new playmate."

Mei Lin extended the back of her hand to the mare's muzzle. The horse touched Mei Lin's hand, bobbed her head, smelled her hair, and nudged her shoulder. Mei Lin untied the reins and turned to go. She stopped and turned back to Caleb.

"What mean 'playmate'?"

"It means that you and she are going to have great fun together. Aren't you?"

"Yes. Thank you. It best present—it only present—I ever have."

Mei Lin led the mare to the corral. She opened the gate and closed it after the horse had passed through. She slipped the bridle off and hung it on a post.

She offered the back of her hand again. The horse touched it with her muzzle and nipped at her hair. Mei Lin rubbed the horse's neck and ran her hand down the black dorsal stripe, from the withers to the tail, all the time talking to the horse, telling the little mare what good friends they were going to be and what good times they were going to have.

Mei Lin looked up and saw Caleb outside the corral, watching her. She smiled. "Thank you," she said.

"Come here," he said. She opened the gate, passed through, and closed the gate. Caleb reached into the wagon bed for a package. "This is for you."

She took the package, looked up at him, uncomprehending, overwhelmed.

"It's not going to open itself, Mei Lin."

She unwrapped the package, and her eyes and mouth opened wide. She handed Caleb the wrapping and held up a pair of blue denim trousers, a calico shirt, and a denim jacket.

"Cay-leb! I so surprise!" She held the pants up at her waist. She looked up at him and smiled. Pressing the shirt to her chest, she checked the sleeve length. "They my size! How you do that? Where you get them?"

"General store. They're boys' clothes. Uh, except this." He handed her a pair of knee-length flannel underpants. She took the underpants and held them up.

"Oooh, I never have before." She reached up and kissed Caleb. "Thank you for everything. Now I can help more."

Caleb and his four helpers worked long hours on the dredge, eager to complete the structure and housing by the time the hardware arrived.

However busy he was, Caleb found time each day to help Mei Lin with the mare. She groomed the horse so much that he didn't have to remind her to be sure there was no mud or other debris in the saddle area. He showed her how to place the saddle pad forward of the withers, how to put the saddle on her hip and rock it back and forth in order to gather momentum to swing it up on the mare's back, how to slide the blanket and pad back into place to keep the hairs aligned properly. He explained how to connect and adjust the cinch and latigo and the breastplate.

Mei Lin listened carefully and watched his every move. She asked intelligent questions. And hard questions. When he was teaching her how to mount, he began by telling her that she should always mount from the left side.

She frowned. "Why?" she said.

"Well, uh, that's just the way it's done."

"Why?"

"Dammit, Mei Lin, I don't know why. That's the way it's always been done. Maybe it began with a reason. I heard that it goes back hundreds of years, when knights wore swords on the left side, and if they mounted from the right side, the sword got in the way."

"I no wear sword. You no wear sword."

Caleb closed his eyes and tilted his head back. He didn't know whether to laugh at her or spank her.

"Okay, you mount from either side. Just be sure to be consistent. If you want to mount from the right side, mount from that side every time. Don't confuse your horse."

She smiled. "I mount from left side. Okay."

He managed to smile.

"Maybe I start wearing sword," she said.

He lunged for her, and she danced away.

Most of the time, she listened without interrupting, but she did not hesitate to ask him to repeat an instruction. Once he had demonstrated a task, she did not permit him to do it again. Her "I do!" was sufficient to cause him to back off.

She was a quick learner. After only a few days, rather than

give instruction, he simply watched and occasionally pointed out an error or suggested a better way to perform a task.

One morning, he awoke to the staccato sound of hooves in the meadow. He looked out to see Mei Lin on the mare, galloping hard up the slope toward the line of trees, her hair and the mare's tail streaming behind. Later, he saw Mei Lin in the corral, rubbing the horse down, talking to her, the mare nuzzling her and following her, and he knew that his help was no longer needed.

On another day, he watched Mei Lin run in the meadow, laughing, the mare running alongside, bucking and prancing like a filly, galloping ahead, slowing to let Mei Lin catch up, running together.

Finally Mei Lin slowed and stopped, panting and laughing while the mare nuzzled her and prodded her back, eager for another run. The two playmates walked side by side to the cabin.

"Have you named her yet?" Caleb said.

Mei Lin rubbed the horse's muzzle. "Yes. She name 'Chica'."

"Chica? What kinda name is that?"

"It Mexican. I have friend at Rat Trap. She Mexican, sweet girl. She name 'Chica'."

"I never saw her at Rat Trap."

Mei Lin stroked the horse's back. "She stolen before you come. Just 'bout two month before you come. Polly very angry. Send two men find her. Same who hurt me. They not find them. Polly very, very angry. I hope he good man. I think he good man. He treat Chica good. Polly begin lock my door at night."

Mei Lin looked away as she stroked the horse. "I miss Chica. She my only friend at Rat Trap. My only friend almost two year." She looked up at Caleb. Her eyes glistened. She lowered her head and walked toward the corral. Chica followed, nipping her shoulder.

Caleb shook his head. *You've seen too much, little girl. Too much. How can you still smile?*

CHAPTER 6
I THINK I CALL YOU "HONEE"

Caleb stood in the road in the middle of Stanley beside the four-mule team hitched to a freight wagon. Three other wagons, each with a four-mule team, were lined out behind. Caleb had hired the wagons and teams for the sixty-mile trip to Ketchum to pick up the hardware for the dredge. Three saddle horses were tied to the tailgates of wagons for unforeseen circumstances.

Word had arrived a week ago that the buckets, steam engine, and other hardware had been delivered at the railhead. Now he was paying for storage and wanted to claim the materials as quickly as possible.

He had considered having the gear picked up and hauled by a transport group that made the run regularly between Ketchum and the Stanley Basin. The group transported everything from mining equipment to groceries.

Thus far, Caleb's experience with the transport people had been limited. Periodically he had entrusted Wally Custer, a transport worker and son of Abel, the general store owner who was a friend of Caleb's, with picking up money for him at the Ketchum Western Union office on his regular runs. With the other transport people, including the foreman, Caleb was singularly unimpressed.

Caleb had decided that he would handle the management himself. He was content to hire wagons, teams, and drivers from the transport group. They had the experience, and they knew the route and the wagons. But he made it clear that he was in charge.

The transport people weren't accustomed to a mere dredge operator questioning their expertise, but they wouldn't pass up the opportunity for the business. They even seemed to be quite satisfied to let somebody else bear the responsibility when things didn't go according to plan, which seemed to be common on the Ketchum run.

The caravan of four wagons from Stanley to Ketchum was a trial. At the start, the road was still wet from a light rain overnight, and wagons and mules slid about, especially on the grades. One of the drivers was nursing an aching head from a late night at the Rat Trap, and another complained to anyone who would listen of a throbbing toothache.

And there were delays. The right front wheel of the lead wagon, driven by Caleb, struck a rock protruding from the roadbed and broke the wheel and two spokes. Caleb tied the lines to the brake handle and got down. He looked at the broken wheel and shook his head. The transport foreman, who had been driving the second wagon, walked up to Caleb's wagon and looked down at the wheel.

Caleb frowned at the foreman. "Look at these spokes," Caleb said, pointing to the broken spokes. "Look how dry and brittle they are. They look a hundred years old."

The foreman raised an eyebrow. "No, boss, they've just wintered over a few years in Stanley. Cain't pull the wagons in the house, you know. Don't fret, boss. It happens. That's why we carry spares." He motioned with his head toward the two men who had just untied a wheel from underneath the second wagon. They pulled the wheel upright and rolled it toward Caleb's wagon.

Mei Lin sat Chica quietly beside the road, watching the wheel replacement. Caleb had invited her to ride on the wagon seat with him at the outset. He was not surprised when she said that she would prefer to ride Chica.

Not a few of the transport workers had glanced Mei Lin's way since the beginning of the journey. Doubtless some remembered her from the Rat Trap. Caleb put an end to their curiosity on the first day. He glowered at any who showed interest in her.

When one seedy character took a few steps toward her at a rest stop, Caleb strode over to stand between him and Mei Lin. "You got time on your hands?" Caleb said. "I'll ask your foreman if he still needs your employment." The man stopped, surprised, and withdrew. Caleb glanced at Mei Lin whose lips turned up at the corners ever so slightly. He frowned and strode away.

During the ascent of a difficult grade, Caleb noticed that a lead mule in his team was limping and ordered a halt. He questioned the foreman who admitted hesitantly that the mule had had a problem a few weeks ago, but that he had improved lately.

Caleb was so angry that he forced the foreman to dismount and add his horse to the team. Otherwise, said Caleb, he would reduce his payment by an amount determined by the loss of time due to the lame mule.

The disgruntled foreman walked beside the wagon a few miles before forcing one of his men to give up his own mount for him. The worker gave his boss a glare that suggested that he better watch his back.

Caleb emerged from the office of the Ketchum railroad storage barns and stopped on the porch. He looked over the barns at the pastel shades of lacy cloud layers on the eastern horizon. The low morning sun cast gray shadows across the station courtyard.

Caleb folded a paper and tucked it into a shirt pocket. He looked across the courtyard where his four wagons were lined up at loading docks. His goods were loaded, and transport workers were tying down the cargo. The workers had turned out at first light and had the wagons loaded before the sun ball had cleared the horizon. Not without a steady rumble of grousing.

He inhaled deeply, profoundly pleased that all was going well and on schedule. The transport foreman had succeeded in buying a replacement mule for the lame animal, so teams were at full strength.

Caleb had drawn some cash on arrival yesterday at the Western Union office, the same office where Wally had picked up cash occasionally. This was the first time he had visited the office personally.

The foreman, standing beside the loaded wagons, waved to Caleb, signaling that all was ready for a departure. The foreman smiled.

He had not been as jovial the previous evening. The caravan had arrived late, and the transport people had looked forward to their usual carousing at the Ketchum saloons. Caleb's announcement of a departure at first light was met with grumbling and not a few angry words, including those of a belligerent foreman.

Caleb had stood his ground and reminded the foreman that he, Caleb, was in charge and that payment of the contracted sum depended on his recognizing this. Caleb added, loud enough for the disgruntled workers to hear, that there would be a bonus if they reached Stanley at the scheduled time. The workers looked wide-eyed at each other, then raised a cheer and headed for their bunks. There would be time and the wherewithal for carousing in Stanley.

★ ★ ★ ★ ★

It was not long before Caleb realized that the journey from Stanley to Ketchum had been a lark compared to the return. The wagons were so heavily loaded now that it was slow going, even on the level. The first day was reasonably easy on a mostly flat road, but the mountain range ahead was always in sight.

The first night was spent at Galena, a stopping place at the foot of the Boulder Mountains. There was a combination lodge, café, and livery where Caleb had arranged the stop. Mules were unhitched and turned into the corral. Caleb and Mei Lin took a room in the small lodge while the transport workers made their beds in the barn. Four-hour shifts of two transport workers guarded the loaded wagons during the night.

The next morning, the caravan pulled out at sunrise. Almost immediately, the road turned upward. On most grades, all four teams had to be hitched to a wagon to make any progress. Reaching a level place, the workers blocked the wagon wheels with rocks, unhitched the mules, and led them down below where the other wagons waited. They hitched the sixteen-mule team to the second wagon and moved up to the level behind the first wagon, then did the same for the third and fourth wagons. This time-consuming relay continued until they reached the summit.

At the pass, wagons were halted to give the teams a rest and to prepare them for the descent. The preparation for the descent was not a favorite chore for the transport workers. They had to find four large logs that would be tied with ropes to the rear of wagons to act as brakes on the downgrades.

The transport crew walked into the woods on each side of the road, looking at downed timber and living trees. One worker shouted that he found a downed tree that had fallen in last winter's storms. Other workers found three living trees with trunks the right size, about twelve inches in diameter. The crew set to work, cutting trees and sawing off limbs.

Caleb and Mei Lin strolled from the road to a point with an unobstructed view of the valley ahead. The forested slopes in the foreground gave way to the broad basin of grasslands and meandering streams. The mountain range beyond was lightly dusted with an early snowfall.

Stanley was visible as a small, dim patchwork in the distance. On the journey toward Ketchum, they had hardly glanced back at this view. Now they were silent at the magnificence of the wide basin and the Sawtooth range.

"Pretty," Mei Lin said.

Caleb looked at her, then back at the valley. "Yes, it is," he said. "We're blessed, Mei Lin. But there's no time for this. Too much work." He turned and walked toward the road.

Mei Lin walked beside him, her head down. "What mean 'blessed'?"

He picked up the pace, impatient to get moving. "That's a hard one. Let me think about it."

They reached the road where Caleb fidgeted as the workers pulled wagons to logs and tied them with ropes to the back of wagons. That done, the foreman waved to Caleb.

"Okay, boss. All set!"

"All right," Caleb said. "Let's go." The foreman waved, and workers climbed aboard their wagons. Caleb took his seat, unwound the lines, and shook them. He moved off, and the other wagons followed. Mei Lin rode up alongside Caleb. He nodded to her.

As the wagons moved off, the ropes that bound logs to the rear of the wagons tightened, and the dragging logs prevented the heavy wagons from picking up speed on the descent. The tactic generally worked without a hitch. But the benefits were paired with risks.

Mei Lin usually rode near the lead wagon, watching Caleb. He glanced occasionally at her, then back at his team, than back at her. She still watched him. He shook his head, turned back to the front. She seemed to be always there, watching. He began to be annoyed by the constant attention.

But once when he looked, she was not there. He turned and looked behind, on both sides of the road, and she had disappeared. He looked ahead, and she was not there. His growing unease mounted.

Then he saw her, galloping in his direction on the back trail until she was beside the wagon. She pulled up, smiling.

"Where were you!" he said. "You need to stay in sight."

She cocked her head. "I had pee. You want me ask you next time?"

He sighed, looked back at the team. "No," he said.

"You want me in sight all time, you want watch next time?" She grinned.

He dropped his head, looked at her, and smiled. "No." He shook the lines, and the mules strained on the traces.

Mei Lin rode over next to the wagon and looked up at Caleb. "Cay-leb?"

He looked at her.

"I think I call you, 'honee'."

He frowned. "Honey? Where did you hear 'honey'?"

"Chica call her friend 'honee,' friend who steal her. She say you call someone you like 'honee.' That okay?"

He smiled thinly. "Yeah, that's okay." He turned back to the front and shook the lines. *Well, it's not okay. It's what Beth called me, honey. Honey, honee, I guess it's not the same.* He shook his head and shook the lines. *Let it go!*

"Cay-leb, honee, you okay?" She still rode beside the wagon and had watched him.

He looked a long moment at her, solemnly. She cocked her head.

"Yeah, okay," he said, "just . . . a little headache."

"I sorry, Cay-leb, honee. Sorry, I do." She turned her horse and trotted on the back trail.

"Mei Lin, you . . . Mei Lin!" But she was gone. He faced forward and sagged, letting the mules find their pace with slack lines.

"Cay-leb, honee!" Mei Lin shouted. He turned sharply toward her and smiled. He had not seen her for a couple of hours and worried about where she was and what she was thinking.

He sobered when he saw that she pointed at the wagon tongue. In his dark mood, he had not noticed that the tongue was rattling and the team's traces were loose and flapping.

"The log!" She pointed at the log that was attached to the back of his wagon. It still slid behind the wagon, but the ropes were slack, and the log was moving faster than the wagon on the steep slick roadbed and was about to strike the rear of the wagon.

Caleb saw the log and the slack ropes. He shook the lines and shouted to the team. The mules tightened the traces, and the team moved ahead at a slow trot. The ropes holding the log stretched out, and the log was dragging again.

Caleb pulled the lines lightly, and the mules slowed to a fast walk. Caleb looked at Mei Lin. He smiled and nodded. She nodded in return, raising her chin ever so slightly.

Later that day, a light rain turned the road surface slippery. Riders on each side of Caleb's wagon tied ropes on the rear of the wagon and pulled them taut to prevent the wagon from sliding sideways. Caleb hoped the other wagons had no problems on the descent, for they had no outriders.

★ ★ ★ ★ ★

The transport workers cheered when the wagons left the descent and lined out on a flat road. Drivers pulled to a stop, wrapped lines around brake handles, and climbed down stiffly, stretching and stamping on the ground. One driver jumped up and down, urging legs and muscles to function.

Drivers walked around to the backs of wagons, untied logs, and rolled them aside. They coiled the ropes and tossed them into wagon beds.

"Now we roll free," the foreman said. The others nodded in agreement and climbed aboard their wagons.

The final night of the journey was spent at the Frank Shaw ranch on the Stanley road. Caleb had arranged the stop a couple of weeks ago. He had met Shaw in Stanley early in the summer and had had coffee and a whiskey with him occasionally since then. Shaw had said that he would welcome the visit.

This was unexpected luxury for the transport group. It was raining lightly when they arrived at the ranch. They were accustomed to spending this night sleeping on the ground in a roadside camp. Now they were invited to put up in the comparative comfort of the hay barn, snug and dry.

Mrs. Shaw was happy enough to welcome the novelty of visitors to the isolated ranch, but she was uneasy about how to treat Mei Lin.

Her husband was not so conflicted. He was mesmerized by the pretty Celestial and had eyes and conversation only for her, virtually ignoring Caleb.

Mrs. Shaw was more amused than offended by her husband's attentions. She knew they would be gone in the morning. She was already curious about what sort of comment he would make about their visitors after their departure.

There was indeed little comment the next morning except for

Caleb's thanks for their hosts' hospitality. But Mr. Shaw was quick to accept Caleb's invitation to meet in Stanley in two weeks time when Caleb would treat to lunch and drinks.

"Bring the Mrs.," Caleb said.

"Um," Mr. Shaw said. "Bring Mei Lin."

Chapter 7
Okay, We Talk Chinese Now

Caleb walked from the doorway of the dredge housing, wiping his hands on a cloth. He stopped. Above the meadow, he saw a dozen Indians at the edge of the forest. They were all afoot. They stood quietly, looking toward the dredge.

Caleb waved. The Indians did not respond. They stood a moment longer, then turned and disappeared into the woods.

"They friendly?" Mei Lin had emerged from the dredge housing and walked up silently behind him. He still looked at the woods where the Indians had vanished.

"Don't know. I've never seen any Indians about." He turned and walked toward the door to the housing.

"I'm going to cabin," Mei Lin said. Caleb waved over his shoulder as he disappeared through the housing door.

Caleb burst from the dredge housing door. The sound of terrified whinnying, almost a scream, sent shivers up his spine. At first, he could not pinpoint the source of the whinnying, but then he saw the horse's bobbing head behind the woodpile.

It was Chica and beyond her was the bear that was causing the uproar. The huge bear had Chica boxed into a forty-five-degree angle of the woodpile. As the bear advanced slowly, Chica shied side to side, terrified. Her eyes were open wide, showing the whites, and her nostrils were flared. The bear also lunged side to side, blocking Chica's escape.

C'mon, Chica. You can get out of there. You've got space, and you're faster than that ol' bear. Break out.

Oh, god! There was Mei Lin running full bore across the meadow toward the woodpile. She screamed, waved, and yelled loudly in Chinese.

"Mei Lin! Stop! Mei Lin! Go back! Stay away!" She ignored him, if she heard him, and ran straight for the bear.

The bear heard her screams and turned toward her. She did not slow and still ran full out toward the bear. The bear moved his head side to side and took a step toward the oncoming two-legged beast.

Mei Lin! You're mad. What are you doing?

Caleb ran to the catwalk, danced down it, and ran toward the woodpile. His mind raced. *What am I doing? Am I as deranged as Mei Lin?*

"Mei Lin! Stop!"

The bear advanced another step toward the approaching apparition.

But the bear thought better of tangling with this strange creature. He whirled around and lumbered off toward the woods.

Mei Lin watched the retreating bear, then collapsed to the ground, gasping. Chica trotted over and nipped at her hair. Mei Lin stood with some difficulty and hugged the horse's neck.

Caleb was hardly halfway to the woodpile when the bear hightailed it for timber. He slowed and walked up to Mei Lin. She looked over Chica's back at him, still gasping.

"Mei Lin," he said, "you're crazy! What would you have done if the bear had waited for you, then charged this screaming banshee?"

Mei Lin frowned. "I not know. I just so angry and frighten, I not think."

They walked toward the cabin. Chica followed, bumping Mei Lin's back repeatedly.

"You better think next time," he said. "That bear could have made a nice lunch outta you."

She looked up at him and smiled. "I don't think so. I taste Chinese sour."

They walked on. "What were you yelling in Chinese?" he said.

"You not want know. Not nice." She smiled impishly, stopped, and looked at him. "What mean 'banshee'?"

"Mmm." He looked up, pondering. "A banshee is a female spirit that yells a lot and tells people that somebody is going to die. I think. Maybe it's a female spirit that causes a lot of trouble. Anyway, it's a woman that is raising some kind of hell."

She smiled, satisfied, and they walked on.

First light. Caleb and Mei Lin stood on the bank at the dredge bow. Andrew and the others stood nearby, watching Caleb.

The dredge was finished. Interior hardware had been installed, and buckets were attached to the ladder. It was the culmination of weeks of construction and installation. All awaited Caleb's signal.

A heavy line ran from each side of the dredge, aft of the bow, to the bank where it was tied to a stout stake driven into the ground. The spud, an enormous circular iron shaft that was secured in a sliding mechanism on the stern, was dropped hard into the pond bottom to counter the digging pull of the bucket-line. The spud also served as a pivot when the dredge bow was swung to the side to begin a new cut. The bucketline ladder, hung from cables attached to the housing, extended about six feet over the bank.

The steam engine's boiler had been filled with water the previous evening. The firebox had been stoked and awaited the flame that would begin the process of getting up steam.

"Let's fire it up," Caleb said. The four workers raised a cheer.

"Okay, boss," said Andrew, "whatever you say."

Caleb walked up the plank to the dredge deck. Mei Lin and the others followed.

Inside, Caleb opened the firebox door, struck a match and ignited the tinder just inside the chamber. Workers raised another cheer. Caleb closed the firebox door.

"Now we wait," Caleb said. The four workers walked outside to stand on the deck or walk down the plank to the bank. A couple of men sat down on the bank and pulled out pipes and small tobacco sacks.

Caleb took Mei Lin by the arm, guiding her to the large room aft of the engine housing. Here was the apparatus for processing the soil dug by the bucketline. "You won't want to be in here once we begin operation," Caleb said. "It's going to be ear-splitting noisy."

"I see gold flakes before when we work in stream," Mei Lin said, "but I no understand how you take gold from buckets of dirt."

"Well, it's pretty hard to understand," he said. She frowned and cocked her head.

"Okay, I'll try to explain. The buckets dump the soil into this big round hopper. It rolls around as water is sprayed into it, and the fine stuff washes out through the holes in the hopper. The stones that are too large to go through the holes are sent to the big belt in the back where they are dumped behind the dredge. These are called tailings. Okay?"

"Okay."

"The small stuff that goes out through the holes of the hopper is called 'fines.' The fines are washed on sluice boxes, something like when you and your husband, uh, your owner, uh, your—"

"It okay, honee. Go on."

"Okay. The fines are washed on through these sluice boxes,

and the gold is caught on plates—look over there—that are covered with mercury. The lighter stuff in the fines is washed overboard. We recover the gold from the plates. That's not all, but that's pretty much how the process works. I'll show you later when we get in operation. Sorry it's so complicated."

"It not complicate. I understand. You think I not understand? Why you think so?'

He smiled. "All right, get down off your high horse. I'll probably be turning over the operation to you."

"Sure. I can do," she said. She patted his cheek, then gave him a playful slap. He had winced after the pat, knowing the slap was next.

Caleb, Mei Lin, and Cal stood on the bank near the dredge bucketline, which extended a few feet over the edge of the bank. Andrew and Larry stood on the dredge deck. Steam issued from the stack above the engine house.

"Are we ready, Andrew?" Caleb called.

"Ready when you are, boss."

"Okay, do it."

Andrew and Larry went inside the engine housing. A moment later, a loud clanking rent the still air. The line of buckets attached to the ladder began moving on the belt, and the bucketline was lowered to the surface of the bank.

The buckets on the underside of the belt dug great chunks of soil from the bank. The full buckets revolved up to the top of the ladder and into the housing where they dumped their loads and, now empty, moved on the bottom side of the ladder back outside. As the buckets removed huge chunks of earth from the shoreline, the bucketline sank into the bank.

The sound of metal on metal and the slapping of bucketline hardware were deafening. Mei Lin put her hands over her ears. Caleb smiled and motioned to Mei Lin to back away. They retreated up the slope from the dredge.

When they had withdrawn far enough to be able to hear each other, they stopped and looked back at the dredge. Caleb pointed at the bucketline.

"See how the bucketline is sinking into the bank. When it has dug down about three feet, the dredge will be swung sideways by loosening the shoreline on one side and pulling on the shoreline on the other side. Then both shorelines are tightened, and the bucketline begins digging again, another three-foot slice. The dredge swings on the spud, the big spike at the back of the dredge. The spud also counters the pull of the buckets digging into the soil, pulling the dredge forward. Understand?"

"I understand. How deep buckets go?"

"Till they hit bedrock. Then the spud is raised, and we move the dredge forward to begin the process of digging and swinging back and forth all over again. It won't be long before the dredge begins moving upstream. We move our pond with us as the tailings pile up behind the dredge."

"I understand," she said.

They walked back down the slope and around the pond bank where they had a view of the side of the dredge and the tailings that were already beginning to pile up behind the dredge. Mei Lin frowned.

"What's wrong?" Caleb said.

"It make mess. It look like dredge shit."

Caleb laughed out loud. "Gotta make a lot of shit to make a little sugar."

She stared at the steady stream of rocks issuing from the conveyor belt at the rear of the dredge. "I no like. It cover pretty pond and pretty land."

Caleb tensed. He looked hard at Mei Lin. "If you don't like it, maybe you'll be content to eat grass and wear rags instead of the groceries and nice clothes the gold is going to buy us!"

She looked hard back at him, turned, and walked away, fuming, up the slope toward the corral.

He watched her go, still upset at her comment, but also wondering at his sharp response. Had she struck a chord?

The single lantern on the table softly illuminated the cabin interior. Mei Lin stood at the cabinet counter, spooning biscuit dough onto a pan. She had been particularly anxious to learn how to make biscuits since Caleb liked them so much. He had taught her, and now she would not permit him to make them. She wrapped her hand in a cloth, opened the stove door, slid the pan inside, and closed the door.

She straightened, wiping her hands on the cloth. She watched him as he applied daubing compound to the log walls from a tin pail. She always knew when he was upset. He would methodically and silently mix the daubing compound outside. Then he would come inside without looking at her and work on the walls without a word.

"I sorry, honee."

He continued without pausing or looking at her.

"Honee?"

He looked up, frowning. He softened and seemed to droop. He put the daubing stick inside the bucket and set it on the floor. He walked to her, touched her cheek.

"All right. I can't stay mad at you. Mei Lin, I don't like to eat up the land. But this is just a small piece of God's country, and we won't be here forever. The land will recover and go back to normal."

She put her arms around him and held him. "Okay, you say so." He put his hands on her cheeks and kissed her forehead.

"Now get those biscuits before they burn, or I'm going to have to get back to the daubing."

★ ★ ★ ★ ★

Mei Lin rode Chica down the slope of the meadow. The clanking and banging noise from the dredge grew louder as she rode closer. The steady stream of stones dropped from the conveyor at the back, building heaps of tailings above the level of the pond. She shook her head.

She pulled up near the side of the dredge and waved to Johnny who stood on the deck, watching the bucketline. He jerked off his cap and waved to her.

Both Mei Lin and Johnny started at a shout from the housing interior. Then another shout. Mei Lin recognized Caleb's voice. She slid off Chica and ran to the dredge, up the plank onto the deck, and inside the housing. Caleb and Johnny stared wide-eyed at the mercury-covered plates.

Caleb smiled at her and pointed to the gold flakes stuck to the plates. He opened his fist and showed her two nuggets. They were tiny, hardly bigger than raisins, but they were the first nuggets they had found.

They went out on deck where Caleb showed the other workers the nuggets. They raised a cheer amid hearty back-slapping all around.

Caleb and Andrew stood on the bank of Stanley Creek, about halfway up the hillside between the pond and the forest. The creek flow had dropped in the past few weeks and now was half its usual size.

"We're not in trouble yet," said Caleb, "but if we don't get rains soon up country, the dredge could bottom out, and then we're in trouble."

They looked at the dredge below. Steam issued from the exhaust pipe, and the clanking of the bucketline was faintly audible.

"Mary's Creek is spring-fed, so it will do for us if our creek goes dry. It flows in the next canyon east, and so far as I know, the water is not used. I don't know of any placers on the creek below, so there's nobody going to complain if we divert part of the flow to Stanley Creek."

Caleb studied the Stanley Creek flow, shook his head. "We need to get that sluice built now."

"Well, I've seen sluices, seen 'em gettin' built and operating, but I wouldn't feel confident to build it by myself," Andrew said.

"It's okay. Go to Stanley tomorrow. Find somebody who knows about sluices, and hire him for the job. He'll have to build a sluice gate on Mary's Creek that can be opened when we need the water and closed when we don't. He'll also have to supervise digging the channel from Mary's Creek to our meadow.

"We can spare two men to help him with the shovel work on the channel. Hire as many as half a dozen others as well if you can find any. Should be a few played-out placer miners around the saloons who would be willing to earn a little beer money."

"I'll git right on it," Andrew said. "You think we'll need the water any time soon? Gittin' near the end of the season."

"Yeah, it is. But I'm still hoping for a few more good weeks before the cold shuts us down. I wouldn't want to have an early shutdown from lack of water. We'll see. The sluice will be good insurance."

Caleb and Mei Lin sat at their usual shady picnic spot, bundled in jackets against the cool early autumn breeze. They ate from plates that lay on the ground beside them, chunks of bread and slices of pork that Caleb had cooked the previous evening. They looked down the slope at the dredge.

"Do you have any questions about the dredge operation?" Caleb said. "I don't expect you to understand everything, but ask me when something doesn't make sense."

Mei Lin bristled. "Why you think I no understand?"

"Well, you don't have a good understanding of English, so I thought that my explanation might not be clear."

"What! You think I no understand 'cause I no talk like you? Okay, I no talk good English, but I understand in head. You no like my English? Okay, we talk Chinese now."

"Xīan zai wǒ mén jiǎn zhōng wěn. Zhē wǒ shǔn koǔ dōu lē yīn wèi zhōng wěn shī wǒ dē mǒo yū. Ěr qiě wǒ xǐ huān shūo zhōng wěn, kě shī wǒ meǐ fǎ shūo yīn wèi nǐ yī gē zhōng wěn zī doū bù dǒng."

She looked up at him, expectantly, as if to say, okay, it's your turn.

He smiled. "Okay," he said, "I get your point. Your Chinklish is just fine."

She bristled. "Chinklish!" She frowned, cocked her head. "Chinklish? Okay. Chinklish okay. You not even know one word Chinese." She leaned over in his face. "Say one word Chinese!"

He pondered, frowning. "Asshole," he said.

"That not nice word, and it not Chinese."

"Well, I thought it was Chinese. You say it often enough."

"I not say now. . . . I don't say now. I don't say it now. It not nice . . . it . . . is not . . . a nice word." She smiled.

"Hmm. Very good."

They returned to their lunch. They looked at the distant Sawtooths and listened to the muffled sounds of the dredge.

Caleb looked up. The cool breeze rippled the tall meadow grasses like ocean swells. The sun was brilliant overhead, but in the Northeast, a cloud on the horizon was darkening. The mass of the cloud boiled, and its edges rolled outward, expanding. The approach of the dark mass was accompanied by a low rumble of rolling thunder. A jagged bolt of lightning shot from the cloud to a distant wooded ridgeline.

Caleb stood. "Mei Lin, get the dishes up to the house. We're about to get some weather." She began collecting their dishes.

The sky darkened, and the breeze quickened. A few large drops of rain fell, a bolt of lightning struck in the forest above the meadow, followed by a loud crack of thunder.

And the sky opened. The rain fell in sheets, blowing in his face as he ran down the slope toward the dredge. Mei Lin ran toward the cabin, holding the dishes over her head.

"Shut it down!" Caleb shouted. "That's enough for the day!"

"Okay, boss, whatever you say!" Andrew shouted.

The bucketline ground to a halt, and the pulsing noise slowed and stopped. The steam engine was shut down. Workers ran from the housing in the downpour and down the plank gangway, up the trail through the meadow toward the bunkhouse.

It would be a welcome evening respite around the stove in the bunkhouse, drinking coffee and exchanging stories and lies.

The hard staccato rain on the cabin roof was accompanied by thunder that rolled and cracked, rattling the windowpanes. Lightning flashed repeatedly, illuminating the cabin interior briefly, followed by absolute darkness.

Caleb jumped at a particularly loud crack of thunder. He settled back down in his bed and pulled the cover up. The room was suddenly illuminated by a lightning flash, and he saw Mei Lin.

She stood by his bed.

He rose on an elbow, spoke in the darkness. "Mei Lin? What are you doing up?"

"I scare, honee."

He looked for her and saw nothing but darkness. Then a flash of lightning showed her still standing there.

The lightning flashed again, and she saw that he had pushed the covers down. She crawled onto the bed and lay down. He pulled the blankets over her. She moved over beside him and snuggled against his chest, shivering. He reached around her and held her, stroking her hair.

Sunlight streamed through the window, casting a rectangle of light on the cabin floor. Mei Lin opened her eyes and sat up. She looked around, as if she were seeing the cabin for the first time. She looked over at the sleeping Caleb, leaned down, and kissed him lightly on the mouth.

He stirred and opened his eyes and saw her. He smiled and pulled her to him. She lay on his chest. His hand moved slowly over her naked body, caressing and fondling. She kissed him again and started to roll off him.

"Not yet, Mei Lin." He took her face in his hands and kissed her.

She pulled back and touched his cheek. "Honee, I love you. I never say before in my life."

He kissed her again, put his arms around her and pulled her close. He looked over her head to the skins on the floor, the skins that had been her bed.

Now what, Caleb Willis?

CHAPTER 8
THE GATHERING STORM

Caleb buttoned his canvas jacket as he walked to the cabin door. He stopped and looked back at Mei Lin. Only the top of her head was visible under the blanket. Opening the door, he stepped outside and slowly closed the door, trying not to wake her.

He looked up at the sky, deep blue and crystal clear, not a cloud in sight. He walked around the corner of the cabin and looked toward the dredge.

But the dredge was not there. It was gone. He shouted toward the bunkhouse and ran down the slope toward the pond. The workers ran from the bunkhouse door, buttoning pants and pulling on shirts.

Caleb reached the pond edge. But it wasn't a pond now. It was a wide, swift-flowing stream that disappeared around a ridge in the distance. He walked over to an iron stake where a shoreline had secured the dredge to the bank.

He looked at the two-foot rope fragment that was still attached to the stake. He picked it up and examined it. Had it frayed and separated from the action of the current?

Not likely, he decided. The smooth edge of the fibers suggested that it had been cut. He looked at the other line a few yards away and reached the same conclusion. He cursed under his breath.

The four workers ran down the slope to Caleb, still buttoning and adjusting clothing.

"What th' hell's goin' on here?" Andrew said.

"We're gonna find out. Johnny, saddle your horse and mine, and come back here. Andrew, you and the boys saddle up. Johnny and I will ride down the left side of the stream. You and the boys ride back here and wait. I'll send word."

"Okay, boss, whatever you say," Andrew said. The four workers ran up the slope toward their bunkhouse tack room.

"Honee, what happen?" Caleb turned to see Mei Lin running toward him, tucking shirt into pants as she ran.

"Well, either the current carried the dredge away, or somebody doesn't want us working the creek and cut it loose. We'll see."

They waited, silent, staring at the tumbling stream.

Johnny rode up with Buck in tow. "Ready, boss. Hi, Mei Lin." She raised a hand in greeting. Caleb mounted, and the two rode at a lope on the left bank along the course of the stream. They disappeared where the torrent curved around a low ridge.

Mei Lin walked up the trail toward the cabin.

"We got us a problem here, Johnny."

They sat their horses on the bank, looking across the stream at the dredge. It was wedged hard up against a pile of logs and brush that had collected in the runoff. The stream at this point was about three times the width of the dredge.

"Seems to be intact," Caleb said. "Don't see any structural damage. But the problem is the creek flow. Runoff's gone down, and the water level is already dropping. The stream is usually just a trickle here. If the dredge bottoms here, we'll never get it back to the pond.

"We've got to hurry. Ride to the boys. Tell them to get the team in harness, and get here as quickly as possible. No wagon. Tell them to come on horseback. Bring all the rope they can find. Pull up on the other bank." He pointed across the stream. Johnny whirled his horse and rode away at a gallop.

Caleb paced on the bank. He tensed when the current momentarily surged. The barge rose slightly, and the bow began to move slowly away from the bank. He cursed under his breath. If the barge moved away from the debris that held it, it could move into the flow of the stream and be carried farther downstream where the creek was shallower. The dredge would never be recovered if that happened.

As he watched, the surge lessened, and the dredge settled back into the debris dam. He exhaled.

On the far bank, the four mounted workers approached at a trot, leading the mule team in harness. They pulled up, and Andrew shouted to Caleb.

"Ready when you are, boss!"

Following Caleb's shouted instruction, Andrew tied a long rope to the mule team's traces. Larry took the other end of the rope and climbed over debris to the deck of the dredge. He tied the rope to the shoreline coupling on the port side of the deck.

"Okay!" Caleb shouted, "take up the slack and keep it taut."

Still following Caleb's instruction, Andrew coiled the end of another rope and threw it to Larry who tied it to the shoreline coupling on the starboard side of the bow. That done, Larry stood and waved to Caleb.

"Good!" Caleb shouted. "Andrew, tie two rope pieces, each about ten feet long, to the end of the starboard rope." Andrew fumbled among the ropes that had been brought from the lean-to's. He found two suitable pieces and tied them to the starboard rope. When he finished, he held the ropes up and waved to Caleb.

"Johnny, bring the starboard rope across! Cal, come with Johnny! Careful, the stream here is shallow, but it may be swimming in spots!"

Johnny took the end of the rope from Andrew and urged his horse into the stream. Halfway across, the horse stepped into a hole and was swimming. At the near bank, the horse found the bottom, and Johnny drummed his heels in the horse's side. The horse lurched up the bank.

Johnny looked back to the other side. Cal still sat his horse at the water's edge. He looked down at the stream, his face a mask of terror.

"C'mon, Cal!" Johnny called. "Just pretend it's your turn in the washtub." Larry, standing near Cal, guffawed.

"We don't have time for this, Cal!" Caleb called.

"I cain't swim!" Cal shouted.

Caleb grimaced, shook his head. *God help us.*

"You ain't swimmin', Cal!" Johnny said. "Your horse is swimmin'. He can swim better'n any of us. Point him into the water, and you'll be across in no time."

Cal gritted his teeth and touched heels gently to his horse. The horse entered the water and walked a few feet. Then he was swimming, and the water rose to his back. The horse was swept downstream with the current.

"I'm goin'! I'm goin'!" Cal yelled.

"The only place you're goin' is up the bank, Cal," said Johnny calmly in a clear, strong voice. At that moment, the horse found footing and lunged up the bank.

"Now, wasn't that fun?" Johnny said.

"Hell, no, it wasn't fun," said Cal, "and I ain't going back across. I'm gonna live here!" Everybody guffawed. Cal smiled.

"C'mon, playtime's over, boys," said Caleb. "We've got to move." Johnny and Cal took the two stout short ropes that were tied to the long line from the dredge and looped them around saddle horns.

"Okay, easy does it!" Caleb shouted. "The mules will do the

pulling, and the boys on this side will pull the bow just a bit away from the bank."

Caleb turned to Cal and Johnny. "Easy does it. All you're doing is steadying, not heavy pulling. We don't want the dredge to pull you and your horses into the stream."

The mules strained in the harness, and the port line tightened. Johnny and Cal moved their horses ahead, and their ropes tightened. The dredge gradually pulled away from its debris wall. It was floating. The men raised a cheer.

Good progress was made as the dredge moved ahead in the slack current. The riders on the near side and the mule team on the far side had to slow or accelerate from time to time to keep the dredge at midstream.

A light breeze cooled Caleb's face, and he looked up. A dark cloud scudded overhead. The sun disappeared, and a few large drops fell, raising tiny eruptions on the stream surface.

The light rain increased and became a deluge. Runoff from the hard rain was immediate, and the current increased. The breeze quickened, and the dredge was soon dead in the water.

Caleb shouted to all to tie the lines to trees to wait out the rain. While Johnny and Cal tied their ropes to a streamside oak, Andrew and Larry on the other side untied the line from the team and tied it to the trunk of a large cottonwood.

The dredge, now in midstream, wavered side to side in the current. The ropes whipped and strained, and the rope on the port side snapped. The dredge, pulled by the starboard line, swung toward the near bank. It nudged the bank and wedged against the top branches of a downed tree that lay in the stream at the bank. Caleb and the others hastily loosened the line where it was tied, took up the slack, and retied it.

The men on both sides of the stream huddled under trees for a semblance of shelter and shivered in the cold rain.

The storm was over as quickly as it came. The dark cloud

moved away, and the stream and banks were flooded with bright, warming sunshine. Everyone stepped from their dripping shelters and looked up. The breeze subsided, and birds sang from their perches on both banks.

"We'll wait a bit longer," Caleb said, "to let the current drop. Won't take long."

At the sound of hooves, all looked up the stream bank. Mei Lin rode Chica at a slow lope, balancing a bag in front of her. She pulled up beside the workers on the far shore.

"Hey, Mei Lin!" said Larry. "What're you doing out here?'

"I thought you like lunch," she said. She opened the bag and offered it to the men.

"You're some kinda angel, Mei Lin," said Andrew. The workers reached into the bag and pulled out sandwiches. They wandered about on the bank, munching on their sandwiches, steam rising from their wet clothes in the warm sunshine.

Mei Lin closed up the bag and walked her horse to the stream edge. Caleb, who had watched all this, shouted. "No, Mei Lin! Stay there! Don't . . ."

But she was already in the water. Her horse walked on the bottom as the water level crept up her side. Mei Lin held the bag high with one hand, the other holding the reins.

She smiled at Caleb. Then her horse stepped into deep water and sank to her back. Mei Lin's eyes opened wide, and she almost dropped the sack.

"Honee!" she called.

"You're okay," Caleb called calmly. "She's swimming and has everything under control. Just stick with her. Everything's okay." He was not as calm as he pretended to be.

Chica found the bottom and lunged up the bank. Mei Lin rode to Caleb and handed him the sack. She smiled.

"I told you to stay there," he said.

"You did?" she cocked her head. "I not hear."

"Of course you heard. You . . ." He looked at Johnny and Cal. They looked on with silly grins on their faces. He dug into the sack.

Mei Lin stowed the clutter and remains of the lunch in her canvas bag. She and the others watched Cal kick his horse into the stream and swim for the near bank. He held the end of a rope. The other end of the rope was tied to the mule team. Once on the bank, Cal handed the rope end to Caleb. He grinned.

"Well done," said Caleb, remembering Cal's first crossing. Not long after that hair-raising event—for Cal, at least—he had kicked his horse into the stream and swam alone to the other bank just to show he could do it. Watchers on both sides of the stream cheered when he climbed out.

"Nothin' to it," Cal said.

Holding the rope end, Caleb went to the dredge, which was hard against the shore and still lodged against the downed tree at the back. He climbed through the branches of the tree to the dredge deck where he tied the line to the port side shoreline coupling. He untied the fragment of the rope that had separated in the storm and dropped it into the stream.

Clambering again through the downed tree branches, he stepped up on the bank and walked to Mei Lin and the others. "Mei Lin, ride up this bank to the dredge site. You don't need to cross. We'll be along soon. I hope."

He shouted to the other side. "Move the team slowly to get the dredge to midstream. We'll take up the slack on this side. Let's go."

As Johnny and Cal attached their lines to their saddle horns, Caleb looked up the bank for Mei Lin. She wasn't there. He looked around. There she was, in the middle of the stream, swimming Chica toward the other side.

Cal grinned. "Want me to go get her, boss?"

Caleb sighed. "No, Cal, she might have to save your life."

Caleb looked across the stream. The water level was down, and the current had slowed. On Caleb's signal, the mules on the far side and riders on the near side moved off slowly. The ropes drew taut, and the dredge was eased away from the snag.

Mei Lin walked beside the team, leading Chica. She waved to Caleb. He frowned, pointed at her, then pointed at the ground. He hoped she understood his meaning: Stay on the bank! No swimming! Reluctantly, he waved.

The dredge was pulled steadily in the slack current and made slow progress upstream. They rounded a ridge and saw the house and outbuildings in the distance. The men raised a cheer.

The two lines on the dredge suddenly jerked taut, and the horsemen and team were stopped in their tracks. All looked at the dredge. It was motionless in the stream.

"It's on the bottom!" Caleb shouted. "Let's put some pressure on the lines, but easy, to see if we can move her off. We don't want to break the ropes."

The riders and the team pulled gently on the lines, but the dredge did not move. As the runoff had decreased, the water level of the shallow creek had dropped just enough to settle the dredge on the bottom.

Caleb looked at the dredge. The slack current caused not the slightest motion on the pontoons. He looked around. Everyone stood motionless, watching him.

Now what? Is this where we winter?

"Cay-leb, honee," Mei Lin shouted, "how 'bout sluice?"

Caleb looked at Mei Lin sharply. *I'll be damned.*

"Andrew, Larry, ride to the sluice. Johnny, hustle across and help. Open the sluice, all the way. Mary's Creek will be full from the rain, and it just might do the trick. All we need is a few inches. Hurry, the water level here is still dropping. Cal, cross over and tend to the team."

I'll be damned.

Andrew and Larry mounted and galloped up the stream bank. Johnny and Cal kicked their horses into the stream. On the other side, Johnny galloped hard up the meadow to catch up. Cal dismounted and walked to the team.

The riders stopped at the cabin. Larry dismounted and collected three shovels from the lean-to. He handed one to each of the others and mounted. They galloped past the woodpile and up the sloping meadow toward the woods, holding their shovels out at arm's length to avoid hitting their mounts.

On a level just short of the edge of timber, they pulled up at the mouth of the sluice channel.

"Johnny," said Andrew, "you stay here. Clean the mouth. Watch for the flow, and don't let the mouth silt up. Larry, come with me." Andrew kicked his horse into a gallop along the sluice, and Larry followed. They disappeared into the woods.

Johnny dropped his shovel, dismounted, and tied his reins to a pine limb. He picked up the shovel and began cleaning the sides and bottom of the sluice at the mouth. The inside of the sluice was wet from runoff from the recent rains, but the channel held no water now since the mouth was open.

Fifteen minutes passed. Johnny looked up the channel. "C'mon, boys. C'mon, water," he muttered to himself.

Ten minutes passed. Johnny strained, searching, staring up the course of the sluice channel.

Then he saw it. A wall of water two feet high, filling the channel, coursed toward him.

"Yippee!" Johnny yelled.

The torrent shot from the sluice mouth, flattened, and flowed down the slope, finding its course until it merged with Stanley Creek.

Johnny grabbed his shovel and mounted hurriedly. He stared

into the woods that bordered the sluice.

Andrew and Larry burst from the trees. Johnny waved his shovel at them. Larry waved his shovel in return. They came up to Johnny at a gallop and turned down the slope toward the pond. Johnny kicked his horse into a gallop behind them.

Caleb saw them coming. He waited, anxiously, pacing along the bank as they pulled up beside the mule team.

"Okay, boys, well done," he shouted. "Cal, come over here and help me with the lines. The rest of you, get the mules ready. Hurry now! The flow from the sluice should hit us full force in a minute. All we need is a few inches and a few minutes."

Cal kicked his horse right into the stream and up the bank on the near side, an experienced water rat now. He took a short rope that Caleb offered. Holding the second short rope, Caleb mounted.

"Okay, let's put a little tension on the lines now," he shouted. "Easy does it!"

Caleb watched the bow pontoons for movement. The creek was narrow at this point, and any increased flow should be more noticeable here than elsewhere.

Move, dammit, lift, move. The flow around the pontoons, hardly a ripple before, increased noticeably. "Be ready, boys. Keep the ropes taut. Be careful. Don't break 'em!"

Then he saw it. The bow rocked the slightest bit, an inch to each side. The pontoon unit amidships rocked almost imperceptibly, but it rocked, up and down, back and forth.

"Now! Everybody, move out, slowly, gently!" Caleb shouted. "Don't break anything. Easy ahead!"

The bow lifted slightly, then dropped gently as the stern lifted a few inches. The dredge was floating.

"Now, pull ahead! We're floating! Move ahead! Slow and steady. Don't break anything!"

Take it easy, Caleb. You're supposed to be in charge. Take it easy.

Caleb breathed a great sigh of relief when the dredge moved from the shallow creek into the deeper pond. The men raised a cheer, and Caleb joined in.

The dredge was towed back to its original mooring where workers tied the shorelines securely to the stakes.

Caleb and Mei Lin watched from the bank. She put her arms around his waist and held him.

"Okay I hug you when men can see, honee?"

He looked down at her and put his arm around her shoulders. "Yes, Mei Lin, it's okay."

He looked at the dredge and beyond to the Sawtooth range.

CHAPTER 9
I KILL MYSELF

Two weeks had passed since the near disaster. The clanking and grinding and rattling evacuation of tailings now reverberated off the surrounding hills from dawn to dusk. The dredge moved slowly up the valley as it gnawed at the pond shore and dragged the pond with it.

The sluice had been closed at Mary's Creek and the sides of the channel raised a foot, more insurance in case it was needed again. It had proved its worth.

Gold flakes were found on most days, but in small quantities. They had taken no more nuggets. Caleb sold gold in Stanley often enough to realize that he was not making expenses. Always frugal in his expenditures, lately he had cut corners as never before. His eastern bank account, which he had long believed would be intact at his death, had been reduced severely with the cost of initially putting the dredge in operation, repairs, and daily expenses.

He had hoped that before winter cold and snow shut him down he would find enough gold to meet costs and finance the plan that was beginning to take shape. Now he was not so sure. In spite of the need for day-to-day expenses, he was careful not to touch the cash reserve that he was accumulating, hidden under the floorboards of the cabin.

Caleb and Johnny stood on the bank, Caleb at the stake for the starboard shoreline and Johnny at the port line. Caleb motioned to Andrew who stood at the engine room door. Andrew went inside. He shut down the bucketline and raised the ladder from the bank.

Caleb and Johnny untied and loosened the two shorelines. Johnny walked over to Caleb. Together they pulled the dredge bow toward them about three feet. Caleb took a couple of loops over the starboard stake and tied the line securely. Johnny walked back to the other line and tied it to the port stake.

Caleb gave Andrew the high sign, and Andrew went back into the engine house. He lowered the ladder, and the bucket-line lurched into movement, chewing great chunks from the bank, beginning again the process for removing a three-foot wide layer of soil from bank surface to bedrock.

Johnny laid the plank that extended from the bank to the dredge gunwale and stepped back. Caleb stepped up on the plank.

"Boss," Johnny said. Caleb stopped and looked back. Johnny motioned with a nod of his head toward the timber above the meadow. A group of about a dozen Indians stood in the shade at the edge of the woods. A few held rifles.

"What do you make of that?" Johnny said.

"Dunno. I hope they're friendly." Caleb waved.

The Indians did not respond. They stood a moment longer, then withdrew into the dark forest.

"You got this animal working in fine order, boss, and it's time for us to move on. We been in one place far longer than any of us likes, so we're on our way." The speaker was Andrew, who always spoke for the others who were generally mute when Andrew was about.

Caleb and Andrew stood on the bank near the bow of the dredge. They had shut down for the day, and the only sound was birdsong and the rustle of dry leaves in the trees up the slope. The other workers stood at the foot of the plank catwalk, chatting and smoking, glancing occasionally toward Caleb and Andrew.

"Are you sure?" said Caleb. "You were in this at the start, and I wanted you to share in the benefits. I think we are about to hit a nice layer of pay dirt."

Andrew smiled. He had heard this hopeful prediction many times, from Caleb and from other bosses. He had been chasing the gold bug too long to put much faith in faith. Anyway, that's not why he and the boys were leaving.

"Well, that's mighty nice of yuh," Andrew said, "but we're beginning to grow moss, so we're headin' out. Cal says he's going to Montana, has a brother in Bozemen. We're bound for Coeur d'Alene. Hear the saloons there are worth lookin' at. And the silver mines there. And there's some nice placers at Warrens, now that they've chased the Chinese out."

Andrew winced. "Uh, sorry boss, but is Mei Lin going to be okay? There's lots of talk."

"You boys have been good workers," Caleb said, "and I hate to see you go. I'll have a little something extra for you before you leave." Caleb looked toward the cabin. "I heard in Stanley about the Warrens business. Don't worry about Mei Lin. She'll be okay."

"Take care of her, boss," Andrew said. "She's some woman. Uh, sorry." Andrew frowned at his own language. He brightened. "That's mighty nice of yuh, the something extra. Just enough to get us to Coeur d'Alene would be welcome.

"One thing I need to tell you," Andrew said. "You know the big dredge that just began working the Pilgrim Fork?"

"I do. I rode over last week to have a look. Most impressive. I tried to talk with the owner—Bennett, is it?—but his workmen said he was too busy to talk."

"Figures. Point is, he don't want to get to know you. What he wants to do is see your backside. Watch out for him. He wants no competition in the gold-dredging business hereabout. He's a dangerous man."

"How do you know this?" Caleb said.

"I got friends who work for him. They don't like him, say he's a mean son of a bitch and plans to destroy anybody who tries to do any dredging in the country, but he pays well, so they stay. Until they find something better, I'll bet."

Andrew signaled to the workers, and they walked over. The men stepped up in order and shook hands with Caleb. Johnny held back.

"Johnny?" said Caleb.

"I'm staying, if that's okay," Johnny said.

"It sure is," said Caleb. "You can do all the work of these yahoos, can't you?"

Johnny grinned. "Yeah, maybe. I'll try."

"Work him hard, boss. He's got more muscles and brainpower than the bunch of us put together," Andrew said. "Sorry to leave you short-handed, but I figure you'll find good hands in Stanley. There's always men looking for work."

"Don't give it a thought. I'll do all right." The men walked away toward the bunkhouse, all smiles and back-slapping and happy to be unencumbered with steady work.

Short-handed indeed. Now Caleb had only Johnny and himself.

And Mei Lin. Always Mei Lin.

He had lost his workmen, and now this new worry. He already knew more about Roderick Bennett than he wanted to know. Andrew had just confirmed what he had heard from the gossip circle that wasted time sitting around the general store stove, smoking and trading stories.

Bennett was an ambitious man, they reported, not accustomed to sharing anything, whether it be occupation, reputation, or position. He had connections, acquired by persuasion, charm, and bribery, and he would entertain no competition to his ambitions or his reputation.

Mei Lin washed the breakfast dishes at the sink. She stopped and turned to watch Caleb. He stood before the pegs of clothing, seemingly deep in thought, staring at the pegs. He took a jacket from a peg and pulled it on. Lifting a hat from a peg, he started for the door.

"Are you okay, honee?" said Mei Lin. "You very quiet."

Caleb stopped, looked at her. "Yeah, okay, just a bit out of sorts. Stuff to do. Need to go to Stanley for supplies."

Mei Lin walked to him and put her arms around his neck. "I worry when you quiet."

He kissed the top of her head. "I'll be back for supper." He went to the door, opened it, and walked through. She walked to the door and watched him climb up on the wagon, shake the lines, and he was gone.

Mei Lin pushed the pot and skillet to the back of the stove. She went to the door and opened it. In the gloaming, she could hardly make out the road. But it was easy enough to see that it was empty. She stood a moment longer, then withdrew into the cabin.

An hour later, she heard a nickering from the meadow. She jumped up and ran to the door. She jerked it open and looked up the road. She saw nothing at first in the darkness, then heard the brushing sounds of harness and squeaking and soft rattling of wagon wheels. She watched as the gray apparition emerged from the darkness, became a shadow, then materialized as mules and wagon moving slowly down the road.

The mules stopped before the cabin. Caleb was slumped in the driver's seat, sleeping or unconscious. Mei Lin went to the wagon. She shook her head to clear it of the alcohol stench, stepped up on the tongue, and shook him. He roused and mumbled something she did not understand.

"Come down, honee. Careful."

Caleb half opened his eyes and mumbled. "Okay, honey . . . home." He leaned on Mei Lin as he climbed down from the wagon. Once on the ground, he stumbled and she caught him. She put his arm around his shoulders and struggled toward the cabin door, almost falling under his weight.

He stopped and leaned back, staring at Mei Lin from heavy-lidded eyes. "That you, Beth? I'm okay, just a little sleepy." Mei Lin looked up at him.

"I missed you so much, Beth," he mumbled. "Where've you been?" He slumped, reeled, and recovered. "Where's Bobby? Sissie? I . . ." His head drooped. Mei Lin shook him roughly. He raised his head and looked at her through glazed eyes.

"Thank you, ma'am."

Mei Lin tightened her grip on his waist and propelled him to the cabin and up the three steps. On the top step, he stumbled and fell heavily through the doorway to the floor. He sprawled on his stomach, arms outstretched.

Mei Lin helped him stand and guided him toward the bed. He fell headlong onto the blankets. Lifting his feet, she removed his boots, pushed him onto the bed, and covered him. She stood over him a moment, listening to his steady breathing. He was already asleep.

She walked to the open doorway and stood there, staring into the darkness. She sat down on the sill, rubbed her face with both hands, and rested her head on her knees.

The room was bathed in sunshine from the window. Caleb opened his eyes, blinked, and pushed the covers down. He squeezed his eyes shut and rubbed his temples, trying to ease the throbbing in his head. He looked down and saw that he still wore his day clothes.

He sat up slowly and looked about the room, disoriented, as if seeing it for the first time. The bed of hide and skins were on the floor against the opposite wall. The supplies he had bought in Stanley were stacked against the wall near the pantry. Then he saw Mei Lin, standing in the open doorway, leaning against the door facing, with her back to him. She was fully dressed.

"Mei Lin, what happened? I don't remember . . . the wagon . . . the team?"

"Everything done," she said without turning.

He swung his legs to the floor and stood. He wavered, reached back to the bed to steady himself, and walked slowly to the doorway. Mei Lin stepped aside. He walked a few steps into the yard and saw the empty wagon and beyond, the mules grazing in the meadow.

He walked back to the doorway and stepped up beside Mei Lin. He looked again at the hide and skins. "I was stupid. I don't remember. Why are the skins on the floor?"

Mei Lin looked out the door. "You not want me last night. You want . . . Beth."

"Beth," he whispered. He rubbed his face with his hands. "I'm sorry, Mei Lin. I was drunk out of my mind. I remember climbing into the wagon seat and nothing after that. The mules know that road better than I do. . . . Thank you for taking care of me. . . . I'm sorry." He put his arm around her shoulders.

"You must love her very much," Mei Lin said, looking at the forest across the road.

He removed his arm and looked through the open door into the treetops. "Yes, I loved her . . . and Bobby . . . and Sissie. Very much."

Mei Lin looked up at him. She thought that she could almost feel his pain. She put her arms around his waist and pulled him close. He wrapped his arms around her shoulders.

"They will always be part of me," he said. "I'm sorry."

"No, it okay. No sorry. I just want little place for me in your life."

He lifted her face with both hands and kissed her. "A little place? It's your fault, you know."

She pulled back and frowned. "My fault? How my fault?"

"I need coffee. Can you make it while I try to do something about this roaring in my head?"

She forced a smile and kissed him. "Okay, you sit. I do anything you want." She walked to the counter and proceeded to make coffee. He went to the clothes pegs and changed his shirt. Picking up his boots, he sat on the barrel and watched her as he pulled on the boots.

Mei Lin carried two tin coffee cups to the table. She set a cup before Caleb and sat down on the chair.

"Okay," she said, "I listen."

Caleb took a long swallow, eyes closed. He set the cup down, rubbed both of his temples, opened his eyes and leaned back. "In the general store, that's the great rumor mill of Stanley, you know, I heard people talking about this federal agent who's making the rounds in central Idaho, checking papers of the Chinese. Every legal Chinese has to have a residence permit. If they don't, they can be deported."

He studied Mei Lin for a reaction. She looked blankly at him. "I thought about you, and I worried about you," he said, "and I started drinking so I would stop thinking."

Mei Lin studied her coffee cup.

"Do you have a permit?" he said.

She stared at the window, the door, the skins stacked in the corner. "I know you ask someday." She drank from her cup and set it down slowly on the table. She inhaled deeply and stared at her hands on the table.

"Every Chinese come here must have paper telling why come. My owner, he say he merchant. He say I his wife. He have papers. All false, how you say, forge."

"Forged," said Caleb.

"Yes, forge. Papers burn when bad men kill Fuhua and burn cabin. I have no paper. I not . . . legal." She looked up at Caleb. "They make me leave now? Deport me?"

"Rumor says the agent is coming to Stanley," he said. "The sheriff and some townspeople say they will help him find illegal Chinese. Rumor is that the illegal Chinese will be rounded up for deportation."

"I kill myself if they try take me."

Caleb and Johnny sat on the bench at the front of the bunkhouse. Johnny pulled on a pipe, raised his chin, and blew smoke straight up. Caleb watched, surprised. He had never seen Johnny with a pipe.

They sat in silence, looking down on the quiet dredge, the three horses and two mules bunched together in the meadow, the dark Sawtooth range across the valley.

"Everything okay?" said Caleb. "You must be rattling around in the bunkhouse."

"Little lonesome. I'm okay. Don't care much for my own cooking, but I'm getting better." Johnny knocked his pipe out against the bench.

Caleb looked up at the sky, cloudless, deep blue. "Warming up," he said. "Not likely to get hot, though. Autumn's coming."

They sat in silence a long moment. Finally, Johnny turned to Caleb. "What's on your mind, boss?"

Caleb spoke without looking at him. "Johnny, I want to ask a favor. I want you to watch what's going on at the house. I came home the other night from Stanley dead drunk. I don't get drunk often, usually just when something's going on that I can't deal with. Sometimes I just get quiet and mellow. Sometimes I'm violent and hurt people.

"This last time, I was just a stumbling drunk, and Mei Lin took care of me. But it could have been otherwise. And I would never get over it. Would you keep a watch on the house when I'm away and when I get home? If you see or hear anything happening down there, would you come down and check?"

Johnny stared at his shoes, pondered, pushed the cold pipe into a shirt pocket, turned to Caleb. "I'll tell you what. I'll come down, and if I see you abusing Mei Lin, drunk or no, I'll beat hell out of you, tie you up, and stick your feet in the hot stove. Will that do it?"

Caleb recoiled, surprised, looked at Johnny. Johnny's face was hard, and Caleb wasn't sure how to read his look. Then Johnny smiled.

Caleb relaxed, smiled. "Well, that sure would get my attention."

"Boss, you couldn't hurt Mei Lin if you was drunk as a skunk. I know that for a fact."

Caleb stood, put a hand on Johnny's shoulder, and patted it. He walked down the hill toward the dredge.

Caleb stood on the bank at the dredge bow, watching the buckets dig into the subsoil. He figured that the bucketline was near bedrock and almost ready for repositioning.

He started when he saw two Indians standing on the pond edge not twenty feet away. He had been so intent on watching the bucketline and listening for the telltale scraping on bedrock that he had not seen them come up. They were lean and dressed in a combination of soiled skins and white men's worn clothing.

The Indians watched Caleb. One made eating motions. "Hungry," he said.

Caleb pondered. He raised his arm in greeting or acknowledgment. He wasn't sure what he meant by the gesture. He assumed they spoke little English and motioned for them to sit. They sat down slowly without taking their eyes off him.

Caleb walked up the slope to the cabin and went inside. After a few minutes, he came out with two plates of food. A slice of pork, a chunk of bread, and boiled potatoes.

Mei Lin had walked out with him and stopped at the corner of the cabin. She watched him walk down the slope toward the dredge.

Caleb handed the plates to the Indians. They nodded to him and took the plates. They ate slowly. And with dignity, Caleb thought.

When they had finished, they stood, still holding the empty plates. Caleb reached for the plates, and they handed them to him. They nodded and, without another word, withdrew and walked up the hill toward the woods.

Caleb watched them go. He shook his head and walked up toward the cabin. Mei Lin still stood beside the cabin, watching the Indians disappear into the forest.

At first light, Caleb walked around the corner of the cabin and stopped. Three Indians stood on the bank near the dredge. They looked straight at him. The morning was still, and birdsong was the only sound. He walked down the slope.

When he reached the Indians, each raised an arm in greeting. Two of the men were those he had fed yesterday. They stood behind the third Indian.

"We work. Help," the third Indian said.

Caleb frowned, pondered. *Now what? Indians working a dredge?* "Well, I need help. I can't pay much."

"No need much. Food and little bit money."

"Okay," Caleb said. He smiled and extended his hand. Each Indian shook his hand in turn.

Caleb and the three Indians sat on the ground near the sluice. Four shovels lay on the ground nearby. Bare soil, some of it still wet, on the sides of the sluice revealed where they had been repairing the sides and cleaning the channel bottom.

Caleb pulled sandwiches from a canvas bag and handed them to the Indians. He offered the open bag, and they took out apples and grapes.

"You are Sheepeaters?" Caleb said to the spokesman of the group.

"That white man name for us. We call ourselves Tukudeka."

The Tukudeka were a branch of Eastern Shoshone. They had lived in peace in central Idaho for centuries, subsisting on game, notably mountain sheep, and gathering wild nuts and berries. They had not forcefully resisted the intrusion into their lands by miners and ranchers, but they had fallen on hard times when their neighbors, the Bannocks, skillfully shifted blame for killings and raids from themselves to the peaceful Tukudeka.

In the 1870s, the Sheepeaters were accused by whites of some scattered killings: settlers, ranchers, prospectors, and a party of Chinese miners. There was no evidence for any of the charges. The Bannocks probably killed the whites, and it was widely held at the time that white men dressed as Indians likely killed the Chinese.

Army leaders weren't too concerned with evidence. The result was the so-called Sheepeater War of 1879. In a campaign of six months in rough terrain against an enemy who knew their country, the army finally won with the surrender of a small band of combatants. The subdued Sheepeaters broke into small bands that thereafter lived in poverty.

"Where do you live?" Caleb said.

"Two canyon that way." He pointed to the west over the near ridge. "About three-hour walk. You come visit?"

The three Sheepeaters had returned to their village immediately on being hired, but they had not gone again during the following week. They had set up a small camp in the forest above the meadow. They had only a rude shelter that was fronted by a stone fire circle. Caleb had provided cooking utensils and food supplies. He had heard occasional shots deep in the forest as they supplemented his provisions with small game.

"Yes," Caleb said. "I would like that. I will come soon. What is your name?"

"Tindoor."

"Tindoor," Caleb repeated. The Indian nodded.

Caleb and Mei Lin rode behind Tindoor in the forest on what appeared to be a game trail. The Indian apparently was a rider, but did not know what to make of the mule at first. He had seen army mules in harness pulling wagons, but he had never seen one saddled. But all went well, and he was content. When questioned by Caleb, he explained that his band had eaten most of their horses in recent years. Only a few remained for use in hunting.

The trail widened and opened to a clearing in the forest. The village was a cluster of half a dozen small cabins, shacks constructed of logs and castoff boards, and a dozen tipis of worn, frayed hides. Three of the cabins had round tin chimneys, but no smoke issued from them. Fire circles of stones fronted tipis. Thin spirals of smoke rose from a couple of the fire pits.

The ground of the village was swept clean, and firewood was stacked in small piles behind each dwelling. Caleb saw a deer carcass hung from a low limb behind one of the shacks. It was little more than a skeleton.

Tindoor followed Caleb's glance. "Deer go away," Tindoor said. "Too many people 'round Stanley. Now cold come." Caleb nodded. "Three men work Stanley, four men work on ranches, but not much money. We have garden there." He pointed at the garden at the back of the village.

In spring and summer, the garden might have borne good crops, but now it was mostly bare. Only some cabbages and squash remained, a few beets and onions. It looked a scant supply for a village of fifty people.

Caleb and Mei Lin wandered about the village, followed by Tindoor. The shy women smiled, withdrawing into their dwellings and into themselves. A few small children followed them, their eyes large and cheeks sunken. All were dressed in little more than rags, though they appeared clean.

Caleb and Mei Lin said their thanks to Tindoor and walked toward their horses. Mei Lin stopped and looked back at the village to see the people watching them leave. She turned back to Caleb.

"Honee, they hungry."

"Yes." He stopped, pondered. "Get the horses." He walked back to Tindoor while Mei Lin untied the reins of Buck and Chica and the mule. She watched Caleb talking with Tindoor and two more men in the center of the village.

Caleb sat on the seat of the wagon, holding the lines of the team. The wagon was loaded with boxes and bags and cooking gear. Behind the wagon, Tindoor, riding Buck, and Mei Lin on Chica drove ten cows and a young bull. Three of the cows were heavy with calves.

Caleb pulled up at the edge of the Sheepeater village. Men and women and children came out, shouting greetings. They wanted to help Caleb down from the wagon, but he smiled and waved them off. The women admired the nervous cows, exclaiming softly among themselves and gently rubbing the backs and sides of the cows. The men and children began carrying the supplies and utensils from the wagon to cabins and tipis.

Tindoor dismounted and tied the reins of the borrowed horse to the back of the wagon. He joined Caleb and Mei Lin in the village yard.

"You've got some grass here," said Caleb, "but you'll eventually want to put the cows on my land. I have plenty of meadow, and the woods above should keep pretty free of snow. They'll find protection there. You saw the spring at the edge of the woods. I don't think it will freeze. Be careful with the three mother cows. They will calve during winter, so keep them close.

"You can build a shelter at the edge of the woods above the pond. I have boards. Build it big enough for the cows and a few of you, in case you have to stay with them any length of time." Tindoor nodded with each instruction.

Caleb shook Tindoor's hand and turned to walk toward Mei Lin. When they saw he was leaving, a dozen villagers followed close behind, saying their thanks in their own language and broken English.

A woman who had walked silently behind Caleb touched his hand. "Thank you, mister." She turned to Mei Lin and touched her hand. "Thank you, missy." She turned and, with arms outstretched, ushered the others back to the village.

"You good man, Cay-leb honee Willis," Mei Lin said.

Caleb and Mei Lin sat on the driver's seat of the wagon. The wagon tongue occasionally clattered as the mules walked easily down the narrow road on a slight downgrade.

"Keep the lines just a bit loose," Caleb said. "If you keep them too tight, you confuse the mules. They might think you want them to stop." Caleb reached over to adjust Mei Lin's hold on the lines.

She pulled her hands away. "Okay, you tell me. I know now. I can do." He smiled and pulled back. Then his face clouded as he remembered young Sissie's frequent response to his instructions: "I can do, I can do." He shook his head.

Mei Lin noticed. "Okay?"

"Yeah, okay."

They rode in silence. Caleb decided that he could hereafter trust Mei Lin with driving the team. Next he would teach her to put the team in harness. She should learn it in one lesson. He had gradually come to realize that she was exceptionally bright and a quick learner, traits that were hidden to him by her Chinklish.

"Honee, you mention winter to Indians. You never talk about winter before. What we do in winter?"

He looked at her and said nothing. He looked ahead at the road and the forest and the Sawtooths. He had said nothing about winter because he hadn't decided what they would do in winter. Not for sure.

Some miners who could afford it closed up operations and wintered in Boise. Some took up rough accommodations in Stanley. Some who had built cabins on their claims stayed and toughed it out.

Maybe he had said nothing because he was struggling with a prospect that could solve one quandary while casting him into darkness.

CHAPTER 10
YOU JUST DESCRIBED ONE OF MY GIRLS!

Caleb stood in front of the cabin with Andrew, Cal, and Larry who had just ridden up and hallooed from the yard. They still held their horses' reins. There were handshakes and back-slapping all around. Mei Lin stood smiling in the cabin doorway.

"I'm glad to see you boys!" Caleb said. "But why? What happened to you up north?"

"Well," Andrew said. "No gold, no prospects. That's the whole story. You think you could use us again?"

"I can indeed. We're hitting some promising sign. Now we'll add a few hours to the day and see if we can make it pay."

Andrew smiled. Same old story, but he almost believed it. He wanted to believe it, coming from this boss that he liked above all he had worked for.

Caleb turned to Cal, frowning. "Cal, I thought you went to Montana. Bozeman, was it?"

Cal ducked his head, looked up. "Yeah, didn't work out. Uh, I don't much care for, uh, my, uh, brother's wife."

"Yeah, that was really a surprise," Andrew said. "Larry and I just rode into Stanley yesterday, and what do you know, we see Cal at th' Trap. How's that for a lucky chance? Anyway, we told him we're coming back to your place and asked him if he wanted to come with us. And here we are."

"And I'm glad to see the lot of you," said Caleb.

"We appreciate you taking us back on," said Andrew. "Now

110

we'd best get that bunkhouse in order." The three men started to mount.

"Hang on, I need to tell you this," Caleb said. The men stopped, holding their reins. "The old boys at the general store gossip circle tell me that Bennett on the Pilgrim Fork is getting real feisty and is making plans to do exactly what you said before, to control dredging in the basin. They say he is going to get real nasty."

"Bring it on!" said Larry. "It was gettin' real boring up north. You got someplace we can do some target practice?"

With the addition of the three experienced men, the dredge operated from first light to dusk. They were finding gold, but not in large quantities. One more cut, Caleb said. One more cut. Again and again.

Caleb walked with Tindoor in the meadow. He counted the cows. Eleven. They had made the adjustment to the new pasture handily. The Sheepeaters had driven the cows back to Caleb's meadow just days after receiving them.

"Bull good," said Tindoor. "I think we have more calves in spring."

"That's good."

"Our people better now with more to eat. Everybody say thank you." Caleb nodded. "People want you come visit village. Can you come?"

"I would like that," Caleb said. "Tomorrow?"

Caleb rode over the wooded ridge and down the trail through the meadow. It had been a pleasant visit in the Sheepeater village. He had been welcomed as a friend and benefactor. He was quite pleased with himself. He was also embarrassed that he was so puffed up.

Caleb hit the road and continued slowly down the slope

toward the cabin. He looked toward the meadow when a mule whinnied a welcome. Caleb looked back at the cabin. He had become accustomed to Mei Lin's bursting from the doorway at the announcement of his coming by whatever animal saw his approach.

But she did not burst from the doorway. He rose in the saddle and looked around the cabin, to the corral, to the tree where they often sat, eating lunch or simply meditating, searching the valley and the Sawtooths. In the distance, he saw three workmen on the dredge, but no Mei Lin. That was fine. He had told her never to go to the dredge unless he was there.

He frowned and drooped. *Have I become that dependent on her? Of course not. Not dependent, just accustomed.*

He pulled up at the corral. He dismounted and removed the bag behind his saddle, tied the reins to a pole. He resisted the temptation to call her. That would be too much like calling his horse, or his dog, if he had a dog.

He walked to the cabin. The door was open. He had not noticed when he rode up. He was irritated, just for a moment. He had told her many times to close the door to keep the bugs out. He walked in and set the bag on the floor in front of the pantry.

He looked around. Nothing was out of place. *Where is she?* He admitted to himself that he missed her greeting. He wanted her here. Now he admitted that he was worried.

He strode down the hill, almost running, to the dredge. He walked along the bank to view the sides. Larry and Johnny saw him.

"What's up, boss?" Johnny said.

Caleb hesitated. "Nothing," he said, and turned to walk up the hill. He stopped, turned back, and shouted. "Have you seen Mei Lin?"

"Hadn't seen her since yesterday," Johnny said.

"Anybody been 'round the place?" Caleb said.

"Didn't see anybody. Heard horses, hooves anyway, 'bout noon, but it might've been the mules in the meadow. They been running around like a couple uh young 'uns. Didn't see any riders."

Mules? He walked around the cabin and looked up to the pasture. The mules and Chica grazed side by side.

Caleb frowned. *Where is she? Walking? Not likely. She never walks when she can ride Chica.* He walked back to the cabin. Inside, he looked at Mei Lin's things. It didn't take long. She had few things. He felt an uncharacteristic flood of guilt. He shrugged it off and decided that nothing was missing.

He stepped to the doorway and stared at the sky. *Mei Lin, where are you?* He looked down, pondering. *Where do I look?*

Wait a minute! He stepped off the doorjamb to the ground. He reached down and picked up a card. The picture on the baseball card showed a pink-cheeked young man wearing a gray shirt with a black, buttoned collar, the word "PITTSBURG" across the front of the shirt. At the bottom of the card, the words, "WAGNER, PITTSBURG." He flipped the card away, thought better of it, picked it up, and pushed it into a pocket.

He went back into the cabin, walked to the chest under the window, and opened it. Pushing a cloth aside, he looked at the pistol. It was the first time he had seen it since coming to Stanley early last spring.

He had hoped he was finished with guns. Oh, he knew that he would have to deal occasionally with rustics who would not let him go his own way. He figured he would likely have to resort to violence to protect himself and what was his. But he hoped he was finished with guns. He wrapped his hand around the grip and pulled the six-shooter from the holster.

He remembered the old stoved-up cowboy who had given it to him in a Deadwood saloon. The old man had looked a hundred years old, but he was probably not over sixty. Bent, bewhiskered, his cheeks more deeply creased than the clothes that hung loosely on his wasted frame, he had helped Caleb up after a couple of toughs had beaten him and left him gasping on the floor.

The old man had helped him to a chair, pulled the bandanna from his own neck, and wiped the blood from Caleb's mouth. He had sat down heavily in his own chair, as if his legs could no longer bear the weight of his body. Caleb thanked him and said he wished they had finished the job. The old cowboy had said that he didn't mean that. He said that Caleb had fought too hard to want to die.

You're a good man, the old cowboy said, I can tell a good man when I see one, and you need to live, for your own sake and to help rub out the bad sumbitches, like the ones that beat up on you.

But you need some help, he said. I see you got nothing on your belt but britches. The old man leaned back and unbuckled his gun belt. He folded the belt over the holster and pistol and handed it to Caleb. I don't need this anymore, he said. I try to use it, and it'll just get me killed. It's done me good service, when I was younger and fit, and I'm passing it to you. I'm happy to know that it's going to a good man who'll use it for good. You need to learn to use it.

Caleb looked at the belt. When he didn't take it, the old man reached over and laid it in his lap. He stood, patted Caleb on the shoulder, and walked toward the door, bent, wobbling, reaching for anything, chair backs, bar, ceiling post, to support him as he walked.

Caleb had learned to use the six-shooter, and it had become part of him. He had worn it like he wore his boots. He had even come to like it, this Colt Peacemaker forty-four. It had once had a shiny nickel finish, but now the barrel was scratched, and one of the ivory grips had lost a chunk from long, rough use. But the bore was still as bright as ever, and the single action smooth as silk.

Caleb spun the cylinder, confirmed that five chambers were loaded and that the hammer rested on the empty chamber. He pushed the six-shooter into the holster and strapped it on his waist. He picked up a sack of cartridges from the chest and emptied it into a pocket.

He reached into the chest again, pushed the fleece coat aside, the wool blanket, the spare long johns, and pulled out the rifle in its scabbard. It was an old Winchester forty-four. He had bought it in Stanley just about a month after arriving. An old fellow at the general store gossip circle had been bragging about his new Winchester 30-30 and asked around if anybody could use his old gun. Comes with the scabbard, he said.

The oldster had reached around behind him, picked up the rifle in its scabbard, and showed them to the group. They passed them around, handling the rifle, their comments showing evidence that they knew guns. Caleb hefted the rifle, worked the lever action, smooth, ran his hand over the clean, worn leather scabbard.

They suited Caleb, and he bought them on the spot. He needed the rifle so he could hunt for the larder. He was glad to get a rifle that was the same caliber as his six-shooter so he would have to buy only one type of cartridge.

He shook his head, and he was back in his cabin. Laying the scabbard on the table, he went to the pantry. He took out jerky, a couple of apples, a chunk of bread, and a slice of ham. He wrapped the ham and bread in a clean cloth and stuffed everything into his saddlebags.

Carrying the filled saddlebags and rifle scabbard, he walked to the corral. Buck shook his reins in recognition. Caleb tied the saddlebags behind the saddle and attached the scabbard. He mounted, drummed the horse with his heels, and galloped up the road.

The Rat Trap was almost empty in midafternoon. Four men sat at a table near the wall opposite the bar. A middle-aged woman stood behind one of the men, fondling his ear. The man looked up, frowned, and brushed her hand away.

Across the room, at the back in a darkened corner, two men sat slouched over their drinks on the table, talking softly.

The saloon madam stood behind the bar, talking with the bartender who was bent over, washing glasses, displaying the bald spot on top of his head.

The outside door flew open, and Caleb stepped in. He looked around, his eyes adjusting to the darkened interior. The four card players looked up at Caleb. Two of the men laid their cards slowly on the table. The men spoke softly to each other, without taking their eyes off Caleb. They saw his six-shooter, the first time they had seen him armed.

The woman standing behind the card players stepped back. Caleb recognized her from his last visit to the Rat Trap when he had taken Mei Lin.

The two men at the table at the back stood slowly, hands near pistols.

Caleb noted all this and turned to look at the bar. The bartender and madam stood side by side, watching him.

"You're not welcome here, mister," she said.

"Where is she?"

"Who?"

Caleb tensed. "Don't mess with me, you dried-up old whore! Where is she?"

"Walk out of here now, cowboy, or you ain't gonna walk out at all!"

Caleb drew his pistol, cocked it, and pointed it at her. "Talk to me, grandma!"

She was more nervous than her belligerent tone suggested. She cut her eyes toward the back of the room. Caleb turned to see the two men at the back table standing. One of the men held his pistol leveled on him. Caleb pointed and fired, dropping him. The other man at the table took a step backward and held his arms out, showing that he had no intention of drawing.

Caleb whirled around to see the madam raising a shotgun in his direction. He leveled his six-shooter at her before she could bring it up.

"Drop it, Polly, or you're dead," Caleb said. Wide-eyed and jaw agape, the madam dropped the shotgun to the floor with a clatter. She babbled incoherently, something about don't shoot, I'm not armed.

The bartender, wide-eyed and hands high over his head, cut his eyes at his proprietor. He turned back to Caleb and grinned.

The saloon was quiet as death. Smoke from the gunshot still drifted about the room, like fog in the shafts of sunlight from the windows. The four card players stood at their table, watching him, cards forgotten. The woman had disappeared. The man at the back table had not moved, except to lower his arms. He still watched Caleb.

Caleb looked around. He slowly pushed the six-shooter into the holster. He walked to the door and through it, closing it behind him.

Outside on the plank walk, he looked around, frowning, pondering, squinting in the bright sunshine. He saw the middle-aged prostitute standing on the walk near the side of the saloon. She beckoned urgently to him.

Caleb strode to her. She took his sleeve and pulled him into the alley between the saloon and the adjacent feed store. They hurried down the alley and stopped near the back of the saloon.

"Listen!" she said. "Mei Lin—"

At the shot, Caleb drew his pistol, pointed toward the shooter on the front walk, and fired in one rapid, continuous motion. The shooter was blown backward and collapsed. Caleb holstered the six-shooter and bent over the prostrate woman.

Caleb held her head. Her eyes blinked rapidly.

"Boise," she said.

"Boise? Where? Where in Boise?"

"Bo- . . . Boise." She gasped. "Ma-ma-datter." Her eyes fluttered, and she exhaled in a long sigh. He gently closed her eyes, still holding her head, and looked around. He wanted to do something for this good woman, this whore who had died well, but he knew that he could do nothing. He lowered her head to the ground.

He stood, walked to the saloon front, and looked down at her killer. His eyes misted, and he kicked the corpse violently. "Goddam son of a bitch," he mumbled. He kicked him hard again.

He looked up and glared at three men in front of the saloon door, watching him. When they made eye contact, they rushed back inside, bumping and stumbling over each other. The door banged shut, echoing in the still air.

Caleb walked to his horse. He untied the reins and looked around. The street was empty. He grasped the saddle horn and stared at the seat.

"Ma-ma-datter?" he said aloud.

He swung up into the saddle and kicked Buck into a gallop.

Caleb rode at a steady lope on a lightly traveled wagon road on the valley floor. Hillsides on each side of the valley wore a patchwork of green conifers and deciduous trees in autumn color. Caleb saw nothing but the road ahead.

He sat on the ground, leaning against a tree trunk. Chewing on a biscuit, he watched Buck drinking from the shallow pool at the base of the small spring.

He looked up. The cloud layer had darkened and lowered in the past hour. Standing and stretching, he walked to Buck and pulled a yellow slicker from the pack behind the saddle.

Caleb rode at a lope, hunched over against the hard rain, his hat pulled down, slicker buttoned at the top and billowing behind.

The flames of the small fire cast a warm glow that described a circle of light that included Buck, hobbled and head hanging, and Caleb, lying beside the fire and covered with the slicker, his head resting on his saddle. His eyes were open, and he stared into the flames.

Caleb rode at a lope on a road that was little more than a wide trail in the forest, a sinuous narrow passage through the mountains. When the road turned upward, Buck wheezed and labored, and Caleb slowed the horse to a walk.

He rode into Boise at dusk. It wasn't a big town, as towns go, but big for Idaho. He walked his horse through a residential district on the north side into the town center.

Riding down a street with shuttered shops on both sides, he turned into a cross street, up the next street lined with shops, a saloon here, another across the street, a grocer where the proprietor was moving crates of fruits and vegetables inside.

He rode aimlessly, not sure what he was looking for. Rounding a corner, he pulled Buck up so hard the horse backed.

"What th—" A dozen men and a few women stared at a strange vehicle that appeared to have dropped down on the Boise street from another planet.

Caleb looked at his first motorcar. The people walked around the car, wide-eyed, some talking softly, others laughing loudly. They wanted urgently to touch the gleaming black body, but every time a hand reached out toward the car, a burly middle-aged man in a severe black suit standing nearby smiled and raised a restraining hand. The hand belied the smile.

The seat of upholstered leather was worthy of a sitting room in a fine house. A gleaming gold-colored lantern was fixed to each side of the curved front dash. Four white pneumatic tires under narrow fenders complemented the black finish of the vehicle. The only other color on the chassis was a maroon panel on each side of the seat.

Caleb walked his horse around the apparition and continued down the street. The car, absurd or portent, forced him to think of the future. *What is coming for me?*

He shook his head and rode on. At the corner, he stopped and spoke to a man dressed in work clothes who appeared to be one who would know something about saloons and brothels. He asked him whether he had seen a young Chinese woman who didn't seem to belong. She would be scared, accompanied by one or two toughs. No, he hadn't seen such a woman.

Caleb rode on, stopping walkers and riders to ask the same questions. Most were not receptive to his queries. They were not friendly, not forthcoming, even suspicious of this stranger.

And why should he be looking for a particular young Chinese woman? There were ample brothels in Boise where surely he could find what he's looking for. Those who gave him any response at least affirmed that they had not seen the woman he described.

His crisscrossing pattern of riding the streets was taking him farther from genteel Boise toward a rougher district. On a dark street, he saw a staggering figure, a bit shabby, but dressed in clothes that at one time were high style. This man surely knows saloons. Caleb pulled Buck up beside the man and leaned over.

"My good man," Caleb said, "where would I find a first-rate saloon? One that has a stable of first-rate, pretty women?"

The man stopped, weaved, and looked up at Caleb. He furrowed his brow and pursed his lips, deep in thought. "Hmm. A first-rate saloon with first-rate whores." He looked down at his feet, staggered a bit. "Now, if I was looking for a first-rate saloon with first-rate whores, I would want to look at a goodly number of saloons that fit that description so I could do a comparison." Hic.

"You best ride two streets that way." He pointed. "That takes you to Main Street. There are . . ." He wrinkled his forehead, searching, counting on the fingers of both hands, "seven saloons of varying quality on one block. I would have a look there if I was looking for a first-rate saloon with first-rate whores." He weaved, grabbed a lamppost for support and looked at the gutter. "Or any kind uv saloon, akshooly."

Caleb leaned down and offered a coin. The man looked up, surprised, and took the coin. Caleb touched his hat and rode off in the direction indicated. The drunk watched him a moment, then looked again at the coin. He sauntered off, smiling, the evening having been salvaged.

Caleb rode two blocks on the dark street and turned onto Main Street. He rode slowly down the middle of the street, then pulled Buck up so abruptly, the horse backed down before Caleb got control.

There it was: The Mad Hatter.

He walked his horse to the hitching rail, dismounted, and tied the reins. He stepped up on the sidewalk, stopped and looked around, up and down the street, empty, and walked to the door.

Caleb stopped just inside the door and looked around as his eyes adjusted to the dimly lit room. The half-dozen card players at a round table glanced up at him, then returned to their cards and drinks and the two women that stood behind them. The women continued looking at him. One of the women smiled.

Caleb walked slowly to the bar. Two men at the far end leaned over their drinks, talking softly. The bartender, wearing a soiled apron over a bulging gut, waddled over and stood silently before Caleb.

The bartender's countenance said: I don't give a damn whether you order or not, so let's have it. Caleb smiled and ordered a whiskey.

The madam, standing behind the piano, had watched Caleb from his entrance. She strolled over and stopped beside him. She leaned her back against the bar. He looked idly at her, repelled by her painted face and blood-red lips. He turned back to his glass and sipped.

"New here, cowboy? First time I seen you."

"Yep, passing through," this while studying the amber liquid in his glass.

"You look a mite tired."

"Yep. I am that."

"I can fix that. Fancy a poke?"

He smiled thinly, sighed, turned the slightest toward her. "Now that would help, that's for sure."

"What strikes your fancy?"

Caleb replied, without enthusiasm, tired, looking into his glass. "Young, pretty, small tits, a little spirit. I like Orientals."

Madam perked up, wide-eyed. "Old son, you just described one of my girls! Oh, you will like her!"

"You're on," he said, looking into his glass, swirling the whiskey.

"C'mon," she said, "finish your drink. "Oh, you're going to love this girl!" He raised the glass and emptied it.

Madam took his glass, set it on the bar, then tucked her arm under his and propelled him toward the stairs. At the foot, she stopped and pointed up the stairway.

"Second door on the left. You wait there, and I'll send up your angel."

He nodded, looked up the stair, and climbed slowly, each step announced with a creaking protest. At the top, he passed the first door, ignoring the thumping cadence of the bedsprings. Stopping at the next door, he looked back toward the stairs, opened the door, stepped into the room. He closed the door behind him, listened for the closing click.

He looked around the room. Besides the bed, there were only a chest of drawers and a narrow wardrobe. The bed was rusted cast iron, supporting a thin, sagging mattress. The sheets surprisingly were clean and neatly tucked under the mattress. Lacy curtains, stained but clean, stirred before the open window.

He stood quietly, facing the hall door. Waiting.

A couple of minutes later, he heard a commotion in the hall, a shuffling and scraping. The knob turned, the door opened halfway, and he saw Mei Lin in the dark corridor. She wore a red dress, white lace at the knee-length hem and at the wrists of the long sleeves, all topped with a collar of pink lace and feathers. Surely it was somebody's castoff. If he weren't so tense, he would have laughed.

Mei Lin struggled against two men who held her tightly by her arms, pushing her toward the room's open door.

"You nǐ mā dē, that hurts! Let me go, chòu wáng bā! You stink, wáng bā dàn asshole! Take your stinking hands off me!"

Caleb assumed that Mei Lin was pummeling her captors with Chinese expletives. The English expletives he understood only too well. He fought the impulse to smile.

One of the men released Mei Lin and stood grumbling in the hall. He rubbed his cheek that was marked with two long scratches. The other man pushed Mei Lin through the door, still holding her arms tightly. She turned around toward the room, her face full of anger, prepared to face her new tormentor.

She saw Caleb. Her eyes opened wide, and her jaw dropped. He frowned at her. She sobered, recognizing, comprehending.

She jerked an arm from her captor's grasp and took a swing at him. He ducked, laughing. He grabbed her again, pushed her into the room.

"Haǒ lē, sumbitch, zhoˇ kaī! Wáng bà dàn!"

The man released her. "Good luck, cowboy. Watch out for your pecker. She's a mean 'un." He grinned and withdrew, closing the door behind him.

Caleb and Mei Lin waited for the door to click shut. She lunged for him, and they embraced. Tears came and streamed down her face. She clung tightly to him.

"I know you come, honee," softly, almost a whisper. "I knew you come." Caleb kissed her and wiped her tears with the palm of his hand.

Caleb put a finger to his lips, drew his six-shooter, pulled back the hammer, and walked to the door. He opened it slowly, stepped into the dark hall. Mei Lin followed.

They walked slowly down the stairs, each creaking step announcing their progress. Caleb held the pistol behind him.

The madam, standing at the end of the bar, watched the pair as they descended the stairs. Two men standing in front of the bar near her turned to watch.

Caleb and Mei Lin reached the bottom of the stairs and stopped. Caleb glanced around the room.

The madam took a drag of her cigar and blew a stream of smoke over her head. "Well, you surprise me, cowboy. Bit quick on the trigger, huh?"

"You said it, Polly." He showed the pistol to her and the room. She and the two men beside her straightened and stepped back.

"Now you and all your lapdogs just step aside," Caleb said, "and we'll be on our way."

At a sound, Caleb looked toward the end of the bar and saw him, the man called Jack. He leaned on the bar, an unlighted cigarette dangling from his lips. Jack struck a match on the bar and lit the cigarette. He glanced up to the balcony above the stairs. A man stood at the balcony rail, pistol pointing at Caleb.

"You ain't going nowhere," Jack said.

Caleb flung Mei Lin aside, swung his pistol up, and fired. The shooter on the balcony fell backward as his shot went wild.

Caleb whirled to see Jack aiming at him. They fired simultaneously. Jack crashed back against the bar and slid to the floor.

Caleb turned back to the bar and saw the madam bringing up a shotgun in his direction. Caleb fired, and the woman was blown backward, the blast from the shotgun opening a hole in the ceiling.

Caleb surveyed the room, holding the six-shooter in front of him. Patrons stood and sat, tensed, all watching, jaws hanging. Caleb reached back for Mei Lin without taking his eyes off the room. She placed her hand in his, and they walked toward the saloon door, Caleb looking right and left at each step.

CHAPTER 11
DON'T LET ME CATCH YOU ALONE

Mei Lin rode behind Caleb, holding him tightly around his waist. Her head rested on his back, and she rocked back and forth with the motion of the loping horse.

Hours passed. Caleb turned often to watch the back trail and listen for any sounds of being followed. He occasionally pulled Buck up, to listen and let the horse blow.

He set off again at a slow lope. Mei Lin adjusted her hold on Caleb's waist and felt a wetness. She looked at her hand. In the bright moonlight, she saw blood.

"You hurt."

"It's okay. You'll tend to it later. Everything's okay now."

They rode. After a half hour, Caleb weaved in the saddle, almost falling forward before catching himself.

"Stop."

"Later," he said, groggy, weaving.

"You goddam listen me! You stop now!"

He turned off the trail and pulled Buck to a stop. Mei Lin jumped off. She grasped his arms to help him down. He slid off, stumbled, almost fell. She helped him sit on the ground, then lowered him slowly to lie down.

She pulled his shirt from his trousers, revealing a bloody gash in his left side at the waist. Ripping her dress at the hem, she folded the piece into a pad. She then ripped off both of her sleeves at the shoulder to make a tie, placed the pad on the gash and tied the joined sleeves around his waist.

She pressed the pad gently to stem the blood flow. He winced, then relaxed. His eyes closed, and his head turned slowly to the side.

"Honee? Honee? You still here? You hear me? Honee?"

"Yeah, I'm still here, my angel," he said softly.

"We stay here a while. Nobody come, I think."

They rode at a slow lope. Bright moonlight cast shadows of the towering pines across the trail. The shadow of horse and riders moved across the pattern of tree shadow. Mei Lin held Caleb with her arms around his body, her hands on his chest, more to support him than herself. He occasionally made a soft moaning sound. Mei Lin tightened her lips, knowing he was in pain.

When the road and the fields were just beginning to be described by the coming of day, Mei Lin reached up and took the reins, pulling Buck off the road and into the woods.

Caleb stirred. "What?" he said.

"We stop a while. Rest." She pulled Buck up, slid off, and helped him down. She supported him as he slowly kneeled and lay down on the ground.

He exhaled heavily. "Oh, this feels good," he said softly. "We may winter here."

She loosened the tie around his chest and checked the pad. It was completely soaked. She ripped another strip from her dress and made another pad. She applied the pad and replaced the tie. She lay beside him, holding his hand.

At midmorning, they were on the road again. They alternately walked Buck and rode at a lope, saving the horse that was not accustomed to carrying two riders. They pulled off at secluded spots where they could rest in woods or behind outcroppings, unseen from the road. They nibbled on the remnants of the bread, apples, and jerky that Caleb had stowed in his saddlebag.

In the afternoon, the sun disappeared behind a gray overcast. A dark cloud appeared in the north and moved overhead. The breeze freshened and smelled of rain. Mei Lin pulled Buck off the trail and rode across a meadow to the edge of a birch copse.

She slid off the horse, steadied Caleb in the saddle, and walked into the wood. Here was an outcropping with a sharp overhang, almost a shallow cave, that should do.

She walked back to Caleb and led the horse to the overhang. Helping him to dismount, she supported him and guided him to the shelter. She held him as he kneeled, sat, and lay down. Kneeling beside him, she gently pushed him as far under the overhang as possible. Tying Buck's reins to a nearby limb, she removed the saddle and blanket, dragged the saddle to Caleb, and pushed it under his head.

She had hardly settled him when the rain began. Scattered, large drops, then a downpour. Mei Lin lay down beside him. She put the saddle blanket over him and scooted close against him, her arm over his chest. Rivulets of water dripped off the overhang, splashing on the ground a foot from where Mei Lin lay.

She was awakened by birdsong. The wet tops of tall grasses at the edge of their cave sanctuary sparkled in the bright sunshine. She reached for Caleb and touched his face. His eyes opened, blinked.

"You can ride, honee?"

He sighed. "Yeah, I can ride." She sat up. "If you'll help me," he said. She placed her hand under his shoulder to help him rise. "With a kiss." She smiled and leaned over and kissed him.

"Okay," he said, "help me up, and we're off." She put a hand under his shoulders and lifted him. He squeezed his eyes shut and winced in pain.

"Sorry, honee. Almost home."

She stood and pulled him up slowly. She helped him walk to a sapling, which he held for support. "You stay here," she said. "I saddle Buck." Picking up the blanket and saddle, she carried them to the horse, saddled him, and came back for Caleb.

"Okay, ready," she said. "Almost home." She helped him mount, then swung up behind him.

They rode on a familiar trail now that branched off the Stanley road. Mei Lin had kept up a steady chatter with Caleb for the past couple of hours, fearing that he was drifting. She was unsure whether he was sleepy or failing. One more rise, and they would see their valley, the dredge and cabin, the corrals and meadow.

Before they topped the last rise, they saw a thin spiral of smoke ahead. Caleb kicked Buck ahead, and he galloped up the hill. At the top, Caleb pulled him to a sliding stop.

"Oh, god, Mei Lin. Oh, god." They looked down on the dredge, partially burned, still smoldering, the exposed frame of the equipment housing reaching up like bare ribs.

Mei Lin kicked Buck ahead. "You no worry 'bout god. You listen me. I get you to bed."

By the time they reached the cabin, Caleb was slumped in the saddle, weaving and in danger of falling. Mei Lin held him with one hand around his chest and the reins with the other.

She pulled Buck up in front of the cabin door, slid off the horse, and helped Caleb down. He touched the ground and almost fell. Holding him around his chest, she almost dragged him to the door. She opened the door with some difficulty and supported him as he stumbled to the bed.

Mei Lin helped him sit on the side of the bed, then laid him down gently. He sighed heavily and closed his eyes. Pulling his boots off, she lifted his legs slowly onto the bed. She loosened his clothing and removed the pad from his wound.

She made a fire in the stove and heated water. After cleaning the wound with the warm water, she made a new pad from clean rags. First applying a salve to the wound, she applied the pad and tied the shirtsleeve band around his chest.

Pulling the chair from the table to the bedside, she sat, watching him.

Caleb opened his eyes. He turned his head and saw Mei Lin. She sat in her chair beside the bed, slumped over, her head on the bed, sleeping.

"Mei Lin," he said softly.

Her head jerked up, and her eyes opened wide. "Honee Cayleb! You awake." She stood and leaned over him. "How you feel?"

"Hungry. What's for breakfast?"

"You need breakfast, dinner, supper. You sleep almost two day."

He struggled to rise. She pulled him up and helped him scoot back to a sitting position against the headboard. "Two days," he said. "What did I miss?"

"Honee. Somebody kill two Indian and two workmen. Tindoor and two workmen fight, then run away when bad men start shooting. They run to woods, come back when bad men leave. We bury two men. Everybody wait see if you want fix dredge."

Caleb had listened without comment, his face blank, staring at his blankets. "I will look at the dredge. First I want to see the graves. This afternoon."

"We see. You get up if I say you get up. First you eat, then I see."

He looked up at her and smiled. "Yes, ma'am."

She leaned over and kissed him, stroked his cheek. "We see."

★ ★ ★ ★ ★

Caleb and Mei Lin walked slowly toward the bunkhouse. Caleb held his left arm pressed against his bandaged side. He waved to Andrew who sat on a bench outside the bunkhouse. Andrew waved in return and watched Caleb and Mei Lin walk to the two graves beside the bunkhouse.

Cal stood at the graves, staring at the skyline above the forest. Caleb nodded to Cal who stepped back, head hanging.

A small wooden cross was pushed into the ground at the head of each grave. They were marked simply "Johnny" and "Larry."

"Those were the only names we ever knew, boss," Andrew said. He had walked behind Caleb and Mei Lin.

Caleb walked over to Cal who stood beside Larry's grave. Cal's face was screwed up, and he appeared to be on the verge of breaking down.

"Are you okay, Cal?" said Caleb.

Cal couldn't look at him. He stared at the grave. "I cain't get over it, boss. He got killed trying to save my life, and I told him he didn't have to do that. He just said git back, and he went for that guy. He pulled him off his horse, and he had him by the throat, and I told him he didn't have to do that, and he just said git away. Then they shot him. Why would Larry do that? I cain't get over it."

"There are still some good men around, Cal, and we're fortunate when we run across one. Larry was a good man."

Cal nodded, wiped his eyes with a sleeve, and walked to the bunkhouse where he sat down heavily on the bench at the front wall.

Mei Lin stood beside Johnny's grave. She looked down at the marker, glanced briefly at Andrew, then back at the grave. "How . . . how did he die?" she said.

Andrew looked at the grave. "He was like a madman. When

this guy yelled to his pard that he was going to fire the dredge, Johnny just went for him, beating him with his fists, kicking at him, pulling at him. I thought he was going to kill him. Then this guy's pard shot him. Three times he had to shoot Johnny before he fell."

Mei Lin had not taken her eyes off the grave as she listened to Andrew. Tears rolled down her face. She turned to Caleb. "I will miss him, Johnny," she said. "That okay?"

Caleb pulled her to him with his good arm. "Yes, that okay. I will miss him too. He was a fine young man. They were all good men." They stood silent for a long moment.

"Tindoor took the Sheepeaters' bodies?" he said.

"Yes," she said. "He say he borrow mules, take them. I say we come village soon. When you can ride."

"Good." He put his arm around her shoulders, and they walked toward the bunkhouse. Cal stood and waited.

"Sorry, boss," said Andrew, "we tried—"

"Andrew, there's nothing you could have done except get yourself killed. I'm glad you did no more."

"They were white men," said Andrew. "They wore masks, but it didn't matter. I would've recognized the voice anywhere. They were Bennett's men. I told you I knew some men who worked for Bennett. We had drinks at the Rat Trap. I'd recognize the Irish accent anywhere. That's who burned us out. I know it."

Caleb pondered. "Hmm . . . let's have a look." All walked down the slope to the dredge. Caleb walked up the plank to the deck. He looked into the engine house and then into the sorting housing.

He walked back on deck. "You boys might have scared them off before they finished. The engine is okay, and the hardware is intact. They probably thought the fire would do more damage. But the damage appears to be just the housing. We can fix that.

Are you with me?"

Andrew and Cal nodded. "Yeah," said Andrew, "let's get on it."

Bennett. Caleb knew he was going to have to face him sooner or later. It was well known that he intended to have no competition in dredging in the Stanley Basin. And that he would go to any lengths to get what he wanted. Now it seems he had proved it.

Caleb didn't have the men to confront Bennett by force, and he had no conclusive evidence that Bennett had been responsible for the arson. So he spread the word in Stanley that he was going to see Bennett.

He would count on the big man's ego. Bennett wanted control of dredging in the area, but he also craved respect. He wanted to be the great man behind the economic growth of the region. There were even rumors that he harbored political ambitions. Surely he could be dealt with.

Caleb tied Buck's reins to a bush near the dredge catwalk. He stood in awe. He had seen the huge dredge before, but he was still impressed with its size, its power. It was easily four times the size of his own dredge. The last time he was here, it had been in operation. The sound and energy pulsing from the dredge had been overpowering.

Now, it was quiet. The buckets hung from the still ladder. Water dripped from the lips of the buckets. The bucketline must have been shut down shortly before his arrival.

Three men stood at the open door of the dredge engine room, watching him. He stepped onto the catwalk and walked toward them. They waited.

Caleb walked on the catwalk to the deck of the barge. "Mr. Bennett, I believe," Caleb said when he came up to them. The other men stepped behind Bennett.

"Willis. What are you doing here? I thought I sent a message to you when you last were here."

"Yeah, you did. Actually, Mr. Bennett, I have come to ask your advice. You know better than anyone else in the basin what goes on around here, especially concerning dredging."

"Yeah," said Bennett, "that's so. What of it?"

"I suppose you know that I'm dredging on Stanley Creek. I got burned out last week. I was wondering whether you could give me any information on who might have been responsible."

Bennett looked hard at Caleb. "Willis, you're small fry. You'll never make a go of it. You're not making any gold, and you're just about out of cash."

"You know nothing of my cash position! How would—"

"Willis, you're a small fish swimming in deep waters. Get out while you can, while you still have a shirt on your back. And take your little Chinese whore with you."

"You bloated son of a bitch! I'll have you—"

"You'll have me nothing." Bennett smiled. "I might solve my Willis problem right now. You might slip and hit your head on the gunwale, fall into the pond, and never surface. Never seen again. A tragic ending."

Bennett motioned toward Caleb with a sharp movement of his head. The two men behind Bennett moved toward Caleb.

A shot sounded, and a lantern on the wall beside Bennett's head shattered. Everyone jerked away from the spray of glass. They looked toward the sound of the shot.

On the ledge above the pond, a dozen Indians were aligned at the edge of the woods. Rifles were leveled on the men on the dredge.

An Indian stepped from the woods, holding an arrow at his bow. He struck a match and applied the flame to the swabbed head. The head burst into flame. He held the arrow aloft in his bow, aimed at the sky above the dredge.

"All right! All right!" Bennett said. "Get outta here! Don't let me catch you alone, Willis."

"Watch your own back, Bennett." Caleb walked up the catwalk toward his horse. The Indians stepped from behind cover, their rifles still trained on Bennett and his men.

Caleb and six others worked from dawn to dusk on repairing the dredge housing. Besides himself, there were Andrew and Cal, and Tindoor and one other Sheepeater. Two men with some little experience on gold dredges were hired from Stanley. They were guaranteed two weeks' work. Caleb still had boards left over from the original construction, now well weathered, which would do nicely for the repairs.

The repairs finished, the steam engine was fired up, and the dredge was in operation again. Caleb still wanted to get in a few more weeks before winter shut them down.

Winter. He still was in a quandary about winter. He must decide soon. The deciduous trees had turned brilliant autumn color and now had lost most of their leaves. Cold and snow would not be far behind. What to do?

Caleb wanted one more look at the sluice before winter set in. They had not needed it since the incident of the loose dredge, nor would they likely need it early next year, but he wanted to be sure it was in good shape before shutting down the dredge operation.

Caleb and Mei Lin rode up the valley to the sluice. The mouth of the sluice was clean, and the sides recently had been smoothed. They rode along the channel through the pine forest to the point where the channel connected to Mary's Creek. The gate that closed the sluice here was in place and in good condition.

Caleb was satisfied. They rode at a walk back along the sluice through the heavy timber. At a clearing, Caleb pulled Buck up. He closed his eyes and sniffed.

"What?" Mei Lin said.

"Smoke."

Caleb kicked Buck into a lope. Mei Lin followed. They cleared the woods above their meadow and pulled up, looked at the northern sky, and saw above the distant ridgeline a wall of gray smoke.

CHAPTER 12
I MISS YOU TOO MUCH

"Forest fire. A big one."

Caleb turned Buck down the slope and galloped toward the dredge. Mei Lin kicked Chica into a gallop after him.

They arrived at the dredge where they saw the four workers standing on the deck, and the two Sheepeaters on the bank, all watching the smoke columns growing, spreading, turning an angry black.

"Andrew!" Caleb shouted, "lift the spud, and untie the shorelines. Pole the dredge away from the shore. Drop the spud hard in the middle of the pond. That should keep the dredge from drifting." Andrew waved and ran down the gangway to the near shoreline.

"Tindoor!" Caleb called, "drive the cows into the shallows. You'll have to keep them as quiet as possible. They'll spook if the fire reaches us."

Tindoor and the other Sheepeater ran toward the cows that were scattered about in the lower meadow near the pond.

Caleb turned to Mei Lin. "Mei Lin, we need to set a backfire."

"Backfire?"

"C'mon." He kicked Buck into a gallop toward the cabin. Mei Lin followed on Chica.

At the cabin, Caleb pulled up at the corral and dismounted, leaving Buck's reins hanging loose. Running to the lean-to, he picked up a can of kerosene and shook the can to verify that it contained a good supply. He looked around, picked up a box of

137

matches from a workbench and shoved it into a pocket. On his way out, he stopped, picked up a handful of rags, and pushed them into another pocket.

Grabbing Buck's reins, he started to mount, stopped, dropped the reins, let loose a burst of profanity, and looked around frantically. He saw the stack of burlap bags under the workbench. He grabbed a couple and pushed them into his saddle's gullet. Collecting the reins in one hand and holding the kerosene can in the other, he mounted and kicked Buck into a gallop down the slope toward the dredge, Mei Lin following.

They pulled up at the dredge just as Andrew loosed the second shoreline from its stake. He had already tied the first shoreline to a heavy length of iron on the deck, which he would use as an anchor.

Caleb tied Buck's reins to a shoreline stake. Mei Lin dismounted and tied Chica's reins to the same stake.

"Now what we do?" she said.

"We're going to fire the meadow as soon as the cows are in the water. We have a slight breeze blowing up the meadow toward the woods. That's good. If we can burn the meadow and the woods above it, the big fire won't reach us. The grass is beat down on the bank, so the fire shouldn't be a problem here. I want to save the house. We'll probably lose the bunkhouse.

"I'm going to sprinkle the kerosene in the grass, starting right here. We'll work our way up the slope and around the house and corrals. Follow me, not too close, and fire the grass. If it doesn't light, we'll have to soak the rags and light them. That should do it."

"Okay, I take matches," she said.

"Here." He handed her the burlap bags. "Soak these bags in the pond. When we light the grass, we want it to burn up the hill, not down the slope. Use the wet bag to put any flame out that burns down the slope. Okay?"

"Okay." She took the bags and dropped to her knees at the edge of the pond, trailing the bags in the water.

He pulled the matches and rags from his pockets and dropped them on the ground. "Mei Lin!" he said. She looked over her shoulder and saw him point to the rags and matches.

"Okay," she said.

Caleb looked to the meadow and saw Tindoor and another Sheepeater walking the cows toward the pond. He counted. Ten.

"Damn!" Caleb mumbled. He untied Buck's reins, swung up into the saddle, and galloped toward Tindoor. He pulled up before reaching him so he would not interfere with the drive toward the pond.

He shouted. "Tindoor, where's the bull?"

"I not see!" Tindoor shouted. "Sometime he in woods, up there." He pointed up the hill toward a stand of tall pines. A wall of dark smoke rose from the forest beyond.

"Goddamned dumb animal," Caleb mumbled aloud and kicked Buck into a gallop up the meadow slope. He looked back down toward the pond to see the Indians pushing the cows slowly into the shallows.

Pulling Buck up at the edge of the woods, he looked into the dark interior and saw no bull. He rode slowly into the thick woods, looking right and left. The smell of smoke grew stronger.

Then he saw the bull. The animal stood rigidly, facing uphill, toward the approaching fire. Caleb rode slowly toward him.

"All right, you ornery cuss, let's go for a swim." He rode forward and turned the bull toward the meadow. Looking back into the dark forest, he saw a faint swirl of smoke in a sunny opening. He pushed Buck into a fast walk, nudging the bull's flanks with a boot, watching what was going on below.

The dredge lay still, well away from the bank. The spud had been lowered, and Andrew's makeshift anchor line was taut.

The cows milled about in the shallows, apparently content. The two Sheepeaters stood on the bank to prevent any from trying to return to the meadow.

Caleb pushed the bull to the edge of the pond where Tindoor urged him into the water with a switch. The bull obediently stepped into the frigid waters and moved into the midst of his harem. Caleb kicked Buck into a lope to Mei Lin. He dismounted and tied his reins to the stake.

"Okay?" she said.

"Okay. Let's get busy." He picked up the kerosene can.

"Honee. The mules."

Caleb winced. He dropped the can and ran to his horse. He jerked the reins off the stake, mounted hurriedly, and kicked Buck into a gallop toward the cabin.

Caleb rode past the cabin and pulled up near the corrals. The two mules stood on the slope near the road, ears erect, looking toward the wall of black smoke rising from the forest. Caleb rode around them and began pushing them toward the pond.

"Just move on, mules. You don't want any part of that business. Just keep moving. Damn, you disappoint me. I thought you were smarter than this." He kicked Buck into a lope, moving right, then left, pushing the mules and keeping them heading toward the pond.

At the pond, Tindoor stood with outstretched arms to herd the two mules into the shallows. Arriving at the bank, the mules turned back on Caleb, but he shouted and pushed them into the water. When one started back toward the bank, Mei Lin waved her burlap bag at his head, and he turned back into the water.

Caleb slid off Buck and tied the reins to the stake beside Chica.

"Have I forgotten anything?" he said to Mei Lin. She shook her head. "Okay, let's get to it!" he said.

Mei Lin kneeled at the pond edge and soaked the burlap bags again. She gave one to Caleb. He removed the top of the can and sprinkled the kerosene on the dry grass. Mei Lin struck a match and dropped it on the wet grass. It ignited in a low flame and spread slowly along the line of Caleb's sprinkling.

The fire crept out in all directions as the dry grass caught fire, crackling and hissing. Caleb and Mei Lin smothered the flames that burned toward the pond. A slight breeze that blew off the pond and up the slope of the meadow caught the line of flames and pushed them up the slope.

Caleb stood, flexed his back. "That's what we need!" He looked past Mei Lin and saw the flames moving fast toward the slope below the cabin.

"Mei Lin! Take your sack and slow the fire below the cabin. We need to move up there and set the backfire behind the cabin." Mei Lin moved up the slope sideways, beating out the line of low flames.

Caleb looked toward the pond. The dredge was stationary, the anchor line still taut, holding the vessel still. Andrew and Cal stood on the deck, watching Caleb and Mei Lin.

Caleb saw the cows standing quiet in the shallows. Tindoor and the other Indian had waded into the pond and now stood in water up to their knees, watching the cows to prevent any attempt to regain the shore.

Caleb grabbed the kerosene can and ran up the slope toward Mei Lin. "C'mon," he said. "To the cabin." They ran to the back of the house.

The grass at the back of the cabin was beaten down, but it was dry and still flammable. Caleb walked around the perimeter of the cabin and corrals and outbuildings, sprinkling kerosene from the can. When he had reached the road above the cabin, he shouted to Mei Lin who stood where he had begun below the cabin.

"Light it! Be ready with the bag. Don't let it burn toward the house!"

Mei Lin struck a match and applied it to the grass. A low flame appeared and spread slowly. She fanned the flame with her sack. The flames licked at the dry grass and moved away from the cabin.

"Come up here with the matches!" Caleb shouted. She ran to him. "Light it here beside the road so it will move up from the corrals. The road will act as a firebreak. I hope."

Mei Lin lit the grass, wet with kerosene, in three places. That done, they watched the progress of the flames. The line of low flame, pushed by the gentle updraft from the pond, moved slowly up the sloping meadow toward the woods.

The wall of smoke rising from the forest darkened and lifted, churning, expanding, black arms thrusting from the mass. A tall pine that rose above the tops of the other trees suddenly burst into flame, showering sparks and burning limbs. Other trees ignited, and the treetops were aflame. The trees at the edge of the wood above the meadow were still strangely untouched, as if they were immune to the conflagration.

Then, suddenly, the line of trees at the edge exploded into flame. The fire spread along the edge, and the entire forest was engulfed in flames. Caleb and Mei Lin watched, entranced.

Flames from the forest undergrowth spread quickly to the grass of the meadow. The line of flame moved slowly down the slope. The backfire moved faster up the slope, pushed by the breeze.

Caleb and Mei Lin were snatched from their trance by flames that erupted almost at their feet. They swatted the fire with their damp bags until the flames were extinguished. Caleb took Mei Lin's bag and soaked both bags in a water trough beside the corral. He handed a dripping bag to Mei Lin.

They stood like statues, holding their bags, watching the two lines of flames approaching each other. They waited, helpless to do more than watch.

The two lines of flames merged. And disappeared. Smoke from the joined line appeared to increase and rise, then subside and smolder.

Mei Lin looked at Caleb. "Is it over, honee?"

He looked at the smoldering meadow and the forest above. The flames were gone. Smoke swirled and lifted to add to the heavy gray overcast. The bunkhouse had been spared. The ground around it had been so trod and trampled by horses every day that there was no tinder to burn.

"It's over," he said.

For days after the fire, thin spirals of smoke continued to rise from the forest, swirled about above the treetops, and vanished. Then a light rain settled the smoke and ash, and the forest was shrouded in fog for a week. When it lifted, the trees were bare, black skeletons outlined against the deep blue of a clear sky.

The dredge was tied up again at the pond edge, and work resumed. The sounds of the buckets dumping their loads into the cylinder, the cylinder rotating and the stones falling to the belt for disposal fused into one pulsating, deafening roar.

Caleb stepped from the housing door to the deck and took a deep breath. He saw three men standing on the bank, holding the reins of their horses. One waved to him. Caleb walked around the deck and down the plank gangway.

"Mr. Willis?" said the man who had waved. He wore a white shirt and dark tie under his thick woolen suit. The other two men wore working clothes. Caleb recognized the two and waved to them. The dandy he did not know, but assumed he was in charge here.

"I'm Willis," Caleb said. He already did not like this.

"Mr. Willis," the man said, "I'm with federal immigration in

143

Boise." He held up an identification card. Caleb stared at the agent, ignoring the card.

"I'm told you have a Chinese woman working for you," the man said. "I understand she may also be living here."

Caleb raised his eyebrows. He snickered. "Well, you're partly right. She was here. Little bitch ran off. Took my watch and a jar of cash. You looking for her? Maybe she heard somebody was looking for her. Maybe that's why she run off. If you're looking for her, you can't miss her. She's riding the horse I gave her. Pretty little paint gelding."

The agent frowned. "You're not helping her, are you? There's laws against aiding a fugitive."

"A fugitive? What's she done?"

"We think she may have entered the country illegally, using forged papers."

"Be damned. She never said anything about her past. Never thought about it. Hmm."

"And you never asked?"

"Nope. All I ever needed to know about her was whether she could cook and keep me warm at night." Caleb smiled, then turned serious. "A fugitive, you say?"

The agent frowned. His look said that he knew Caleb was lying. The two other men, Stanley men, smiled at Caleb behind the agent's back.

Caleb had learned about the federal agent with only an hour's advance notice. A grizzled member of the gossip circle at the general store, the same who had sold him the rifle, had overheard the agent talking at the saloon and had ridden hard for Caleb's claim. He had passed the agent and the two Stanley men on the road. The Stanley men had been willing to ride with the agent who offered them a half-day's wages just to show him the road.

The friend told Caleb that he would take a circuitous route back to Stanley to avoid being seen by the agent. He had hardly ridden from sight when Caleb told Mei Lin to get ready for the road. Caleb had saddled Chica while Mei Lin packed a saddlebag. She kissed him and hugged him, then mounted Chica and galloped up the slope. He watched until she disappeared into the forest. She would be safe with the Sheepeaters.

Caleb stood on the bank downstream from the dredge at a still backwater of the pond. He wore a fleece jacket and a scarf about his neck. His hat was pulled down to his ears.

He looked down at the pond edge. A thin film of ice extended from the shore about three feet into the pond. He prodded the ice with a stick. It broke up into tiny slivers that floated away from the bank.

He looked up at the sky, a snow sky. Small flakes swirled about in the breeze. A dusting of snow lay on the bank and slope.

Then he saw Mei Lin. She rode at a lope down the meadow, her heavy jacket buttoned at the top and collar raised, and around her neck a scarf that flew out behind her, bouncing with the gait of the horse. She wore no hat, and her hair flew in all directions. She waved to Caleb.

He waved and suddenly was warm. The three days had dragged, and he realized how much he had grown accustomed to having her at his side and in his bed.

She pulled up and slid off Chica. She ran to him and collided hard, forcing him to stumble backward to avoid falling. He never learned. They embraced and kissed.

"I miss you too much," she said.

"I missed you too. All okay in the village?"

"Yes, everything okay. They have enough food, not plenty, but enough, and they have firewood for winter. They okay. I take care of Chica, and I come back."

She kissed him again, mounted, and kicked Chica into a lope up the slope toward the cabin.

The cabin was dark, illuminated only by the faint shaft of moonlight from the window. Caleb lay on his side, the covers pulled up to his chin. His mind raced, remembering the night. Mei Lin's face was a foot from his own. He could feel her steady exhalations lightly caress his face and hear the faint sound, almost a whimper, with each breath.

They had made love earlier, and when it was over they had collapsed on their pillows. She had noticed his misty eyes and had risen on an elbow to look at him.

"What wrong, honee? You okay?" she had said. He had stroked her cheek and kissed her softly on her lips and closed her eyes with a hand.

No, he was not okay. His thoughts were increasingly about Mei Lin. Was he putting her in danger by keeping her? The movement to rid Idaho of the Chinese was intensifying. Legal action was the norm, but on occasion, malcontents became violent. There had been deaths. The whole Chinese population of Warrens, a majority of the town's inhabitants, had been forced to leave with only what they could carry in saddlebags.

Caleb turned to lie on his back and stared at the ceiling.

Caleb walked to the dredge and went aboard. Inside the housing, he saw Andrew, Cal, and Tindoor standing near the boiler. They wore heavy jackets and thick scarves, but the cold and their obvious discomfort convinced Caleb that a decision had to be made. Now.

Caleb was not surprised by the snow. Winter was late this year, but the heavy cloud cover foretold the approaching storm. They had to secure the dredge before the cold and snow made work on the dredge impossible.

He gave the order to begin shutting down the dredge for winter. The others set about their tasks, whether from relief or foreboding, Caleb could not tell.

He had worried about winter for weeks. What to do with the dredge and with themselves? He knew that he should have decided and made plans long ago, but he was torn between options.

Caleb and the others stood on the pond edge. The quiet was almost complete, disconcerting, broken only by birdsong, wind in the pines, ringing in the ears of those who had worked inside the dredge housing. The ringing was only temporary, they said, they hoped.

They were quiet at first, reluctant to talk about uncertain tomorrows. Andrew finally said that he and Cal would go their separate ways, what they had done in previous winters. Maybe to Boise or Challis, maybe just tough it out in Stanley. People did live in Stanley over the winter. The Sheepeaters would return to their village and prepare for winter, exactly as they and their people had done from the beginning of memory.

"Andrew, Cal," Caleb said, "if you have no place definite to go, or people you want to spend winter with, why don't you stay here? You could winterize the bunkhouse, and we'll load it up with provisions. You could watch the stock and the dredge. I don't suppose the dredge will need much watching. It'll be froze solid."

"Sounds like it might be a fit, boss," said Andrew. "Much obliged. Sure would be cheaper than going someplace else. Let me and Cal talk it over and let you know."

Andrew and Cal glanced at each other, a knowing glance, which said that the boss had finally and surely, whether intended or not, announced that he and Mae Lin would not be spending their winter on the claim. Andrew and Cal had speculated at great length on that question.

Caleb nodded. "Take your time. Nothing's going to happen for a while."

And Caleb? He had finally decided. He said nothing to Mei Lin though he suspected that she knew he had plans for winter. Each time she asked about what they would do, where they would be, he had found ways to avoid answering. There would be time for that. Time for announcing, time for explaining, and time for reflection. Time for regretting.

CHAPTER 13
I LOVE YOU HONEE

Caleb and Mei Lin stood in front of the cabin with Andrew and Cal and Tindoor and two other Sheepeaters. All wore thick jackets and hats. Some wore heavy gloves. The sky was clear and still at the moment, but the low dark cloud promised snow and a further drop in the temperature.

Caleb and Mei Lin gave the Sheepeaters two sacks of provisions and thanked them for their hospitality when Mei Lin had ridden to their village ahead of the federal agent's arrival. Tindoor assured Caleb that they had winterized the rough dwelling at the edge of the forest above the meadow where they would stay occasionally when tending the cows.

Thanks and handshakes all around, and the Sheepeaters were gone. They walked through the meadow toward the forest above. A small flurry of snowflakes materialized and seemed to hover and swirl above their heads.

"Ready for the big freeze, boys?" said Caleb to Andrew and Cal.

"Gettin' there," Andrew said.

Andrew and Cal had decided to stick it out on the claim and had been busy winterizing the bunkhouse. They had spent hours at the edge of the forest above the meadow, shirtless in the freezing temperature, cutting burned trees, sawing and splitting the dry wood into lengths to feed the sheepherder stove. They hauled wagonloads of the firewood down to the bunkhouse and stacked it under a newly built lean-to. The roof of the lean-to connected with a roofed walk to the bunkhouse door. Now they would not have to trudge through snow to reach the woodpile.

"So far as I know, just one more chore. Just need to do a bit more caulking to keep the cold on the outside. C'mon, Cal. Let's get on it." Andrew and Cal waved and walked up the slope toward the bunkhouse. Their footsteps were clearly outlined in the light snowfall.

Caleb and Mei Lin silently watched the two men, small snowflakes drifting and swirling, until they went inside the bunkhouse. She turned to him.

"Now, Cay-leb honee. You will tell me." She did not smile.

How do I do this? He replied to her stern look with a blank face. Then he relaxed and smiled.

"I wanted it to be a surprise. We're going to Seattle."

Her jaw dropped, and her eyes opened wide. She cocked her head. "Seattle? Why we go Seattle? What we do in Seattle? How we go Seattle?"

He took her arm and took a step toward the cabin door. "Let's go inside. I need some coffee."

She stood her ground and pulled away from his hand. "Honee, every time you want talk 'bout something hard, you say 'C'mon, I need coffee'."

He laughed. "Do I? Let's go in. We'll talk." He stepped up on the stoop and opened the door. She looked after him, unsmiling. He motioned inside with a movement of his head. She stepped through the door, head down, grim.

They sat at the table, each holding the handle of a mug. He took a sip of coffee. "I thought you would enjoy the trip. We'll ride the train, and we'll stay in a hotel. We'll walk along the seafront. Maybe we'll see the dock where you arrived from China."

"I no want see that place. . . . Why we go Seattle?"

He looked through the window. "I need to see a shipper. I've been told that he can supply dredge hardware cheaper than having it shipped overland or around the Horn."

"What dredge hardware you need?"

He shifted on his keg. "Well, none just now. I just wanted to make this contact, in case I should need something in the future. And we need someplace to winter. And I want to show you a good time." He smiled thinly.

She relaxed, seeming to droop. "Okay, I just . . . I get scared, anything new. Thing I no . . . don't . . . understand."

He scooted his keg over beside her. He took her in his arms and held her. "I just want you to be happy," he said softly, "this year and next year and the next year." He did not add what he really meant, what had tormented him for months. He wanted her to be safe.

She leaned back and looked at him. "I love you, honee. You know that."

Caleb pulled her to him again and rested his head on hers so she could not see his tears. He stared through the window. "Yes, I know that."

Caleb and Mei Lin stood beside the table, looking about the room. He touched the stove again, checking for the third time that the fire was out, and the stove was cold. The cabin was in good order. All that needed stowing was stowed. He slid the window curtain on its pole, darkening the room. Sunlight and cold air flowed through the open doorway.

Caleb picked up the two suitcases. He looked around the room again, wondering silently when and in what condition he would return.

Mei Lin grasped the handle of her suitcase. "I take my case." Caleb looked at her in surprise. "I never have case before," she said. "Always sack or box." He released his hold on the case.

They walked through the door to the yard. Andrew sat in the

driver seat of the wagon. The two mules shifted in the harness. Andrew smiled. Cal sat his horse on the far side of the wagon. He removed the cigarette from his lips quickly, like the little boy caught smoking, and waved.

Caleb nodded. He pulled the door shut and dropped the latch. He stood on the step a moment, staring at the weathered planks of the door.

"Morning, boss, Mei Lin," Andrew said. "Beautiful day for a drive." Caleb turned around and walked to the wagon. He waved to the men.

The day had dawned clear and cold. Yesterday's snow had left but an inch or two on the ground.

"We're getting you on the road just in time," Andrew said. "Weather should hold till we get back. Might be a bit of a chore getting over the pass, but we should make it fine."

Caleb nodded. He tossed his bag into the wagon bed beside Andrew's and Cal's saddlebags. He reached for Mei Lin's bag. She ignored him and swung her bag back and forth, as Caleb had taught her to swing her saddle, and tossed the bag over the sideboards into the bed. She smiled smugly.

She let Caleb boost her up to the wagon seat, and he followed. Andrew shook the lines, and they moved up the road. Cal pulled his horse into line behind the wagon.

Caleb turned his coat collar up and buttoned the top button. He reached over and pulled Mei Lin's collar up. She turned to look at him, her face blank. He could usually read her expressions, but he had not seen this face before.

He stared into the forest beside the road. He was not looking forward to this trip. He had reached a decision just two weeks ago. He had retrieved the sack of cash hidden beneath the cabin floorboards and had gone to Stanley where he sold his small stash of flakes and booked the train tickets. He would have many daylight hours during the trip from Ketchum to Seattle.

He would have to talk with Mei Lin.

What am I going to talk about? When will I tell her? How am I going to tell her?

The first night on the drive was spent at the Shaw Ranch. Caleb had arranged the previous week for overnights at the ranch and the lodge at Galena.

Frank Shaw was delighted to welcome the visitors. He said his hellos to the three men, then ignored them. He insisted on carrying Mei Lin's suitcase as his wife showed their guests to their rooms.

In the sitting room after dinner, Mr. Shaw had eyes and conversation only for Mei Lin. He served her tea, sat opposite her, and talked only with her. Mei Lin was a bit embarrassed by the attention, but she accepted it graciously while trying unsuccessfully to draw the others into the conversation.

Mrs. Shaw smiled at Caleb behind her husband's back, a what-do-you-expect smile. She had known what to expect, remembering the last time Caleb and Mei Lin had stayed with them.

The next morning, Mrs. Shaw and Caleb stood on the front porch, watching Mr. Shaw help Mei Lin climb up to the wagon seat. After seeing her settled, he picked up her suitcase, which he had carried from the house, and deposited it in the wagon bed.

"The old goat likes kittens, puppies, and young women," Mrs. Shaw said to Caleb. "He's harmless."

They spent the second night at the Galena lodge. Andrew and Cal were pleased that they were given a room in the lodge rather than having to put up in the barn, though they were not at all pleased when they were told that they would have to share the room's only bed. Cal opted to sleep on the couch.

★　★　★　★　★

Andrew pulled the mules up beside the standing train. They had reached Ketchum without mishap. The drive to Ketchum was easier than the regular freight runs since the wagon was almost empty, and the mules were frisky from little work. The weather had been tolerable, and the road was dry.

Andrew wrapped the lines around the brake handle and jumped down. He strode around the wagon as Caleb climbed down. Caleb took Mae Lin's hand and supported her as she leaned over and then jumped to the ground. Andrew took the two bags from the wagon bed and set them on the ground beside the wagon. Cal dismounted and tied his reins to the back of the wagon.

Caleb turned to the two men. "We've got a while before we have to board, but you boys better get something to eat in a hurry and move out. You may get some weather on the way home."

"Yeah, okay, boss," Andrew said, "whatever you say."

They looked up at the heavy cloud layer that had darkened and lowered since setting out that morning from the Galena lodge. A few small snowflakes drifted to and fro in the light breeze that swirled about the train yard.

"We'll do fine," Andrew said. "If we get caught by snow, we may just stay at the Galena place and drink beer till thaw." Cal guffawed and sobered quickly, embarrassed. The others smiled.

Caleb shook their hands, patted each on the back. They said goodbye to Mei Lin, each with something between a nod and a bow. She smiled and said goodbye to them. They backed up a few steps, then turned and walked away, Andrew to the wagon and Cal to his horse.

Caleb and Mei Lin stood silently, their bags at their feet, and watched them set out. Caleb glanced at Mei Lin. She still watched, her face expressionless.

"C'mon, let's get coffee," he said, reaching for the bags.

"C'mon, let's get coffee," Mei Lin said, frowning. "Something goin' to happen." She looked up at him, her face a mask. Then she smiled, a smile without warmth. He picked up the bags and walked toward the café across the yard from the train.

They sat in the last seat against the rear wall of the coach, Mei Lin at the window and Caleb in the aisle seat. She leaned against the pane and watched the countryside flash by. Sagebrush, telegraph poles, a fence line, a few scattered cows, an occasional pine, a cedar.

Eyes opened wide and jaw hanging, she turned abruptly to look at him. He smiled, wondering at how little she knew of the world, wondering at her eagerness to discover and absorb new things while his mind had long ago closed. She turned back to look again through the window.

He looked her over and smiled. She was stylishly dressed in a straight gray hobble skirt that reached just above her shoe tops. Over the skirt, she wore a slim jacket of the same color.

He had been relieved to read in the Sears Roebuck catalog that corsets and bustles were no longer the rage. He knew that Mei Lin would have refused that nonsense.

With the help of the Stanley general store owner, Caleb had ordered the clothes two months ago from the Sears catalog. At the time, he had simply wanted her to have clothes fit to come to Stanley or any other Idaho town. Now she would wear her fine clothes in Seattle.

Caleb glanced around the coach. The seats were no more than half filled. Seats faced each other, so perfect strangers were forced to either befriend those sitting opposite or endure hours of silence. Or endure their private conversation.

Caleb studied the older couple facing them on the opposite

seat. They were dressed as if they were prepared for church. Or a wake.

The man wore a black suit with cuffed trousers, a tall collar that was once white, and a wide gray tie. His jacket was flecked with breakfast crumbs. His wife wore a long, severe black dress that projected starched frills up to her chin and ears. She had a look of bewilderment, thought Caleb, or stupidity.

They stared at Mei Lin, without any attempt to mask their stares. The man frowned, his mouth turned down into an inverted bowl. Caleb wondered whether he had ever smiled.

Mei Lin turned from the window to Caleb with a contented look on her face. She sighed and took his arm, pulled him to her, and leaned against his shoulder.

The woman straightened. "Well, I never!" She leaned toward Caleb. "She certainly takes liberties. Does she speak English?"

Caleb put on a thoughtful face, forehead furrowed. He pulled back from Mei Lin, looked grimly at her, then turned and spoke to the woman. "Hmm. I don't know. I must ask." He leaned back, pursed his lips, and spoke to Mei Lin.

"Do you speak English?"

Mei Lin pondered, frowning. She leaned back and replied stiffly and slowly to Caleb, ignoring the man and woman. "Only if I speak to a person who understand proper English," she said. "You understand good English, I think, honee."

The woman's jaw dropped. "Well! Well! I never!" She stood stiffly and glared down at her husband. "Wilbur!"

Wilbur pulled a face that said either, "Sorry," or "I never!" Caleb couldn't decide which. Wilbur stood, and with a "Yes, dear," the pair shuffled up the aisle, bouncing against seats on each side with the rhythm of the train.

"Funny," said Mei Lin, smiling.

"Prigs," said Caleb.

She laughed, sobered, turned to Caleb. "What mean 'prigs'?"

"Prudish . . . uh . . ." He stared at the ceiling. "Somebody who doesn't know how to have fun and doesn't like to see others having fun. Something like that."

"I understand."

She looked back through the window. The rolling land was brown and arid, covered with sage and black lava basalt, broken occasionally by ravines that were crossed on bridges. Mountains were visible in the distance, their slopes covered with green conifers and peaks topped with snow.

The train stood at the station in Boise. Caleb and Mei Lin looked through the window at the platform.

Steam issued from the engine ahead, billowing, obscuring people on the platform. A woman turned away from the steam and waved her hand before her face. The little girl beside her mother stretched her arms out horizontally on each side and tilted her head back, smiling, eyes closed, inhaling the wondrous mechanical fog.

An elderly woman nearby hugged a young man briefly, turned, and took the young woman beside him in her arms and held her tightly. Tears flowed down the young woman's cheeks. The older woman wiped the tears with a hand and kissed the cheek. She picked up a traveling bag and walked to the coach door. The young woman, hands at her cheeks, leaned on her husband who put an arm around her shoulders.

Others on the platform said their goodbyes, shook hands and hugged and kissed, waved. That ritual done, the travelers walked to the coach doors, luggage and bags in hand. They stood aside for arriving passengers to step down from the train, carrying bags and sacks.

Caleb pulled his watch from a vest pocket and looked at it. He returned the watch to the pocket and turned to Mei Lin.

"Would you like to walk on the platform, stretch your legs?" he said.

She bent to look through the window at the platform. "No. I don't like Boise. You go, if you want. I stay here."

"I understand. Okay, just a couple of minutes." He stood and walked to the door behind their seats.

He started to step down from the coach, then stopped and stepped back for a man who was boarding. The man's head was down, looking at the steps, and did not see Caleb. He looked up, saw Caleb, and pushed the round, steel-rimmed glasses up on his nose. He nodded and boarded. Caleb nodded in return and stepped down to the platform.

Caleb walked briskly up the platform and stopped beside the engine. He marveled at the intricate structure, gleaming surfaces, and churning steam.

"Booooard!" Two coaches back, the conductor hung from a door, holding a flag. Caleb hurried toward his coach at the rear. Passing the conductor, he raised a hand in salute.

"Don't leave me!" Caleb said, smiling.

The conductor frowned. "Time and this train waits for no one." He smiled.

Caleb quickened his pace, running now. "Goddamned philosopher," he mumbled to himself. "Or a philosophical god. At least, he's god on this train."

Caleb reached his door at the rear of the last coach. He grabbed the bar and swung up the step to the floor, just as the engine chugged into life, and the train began moving.

He stepped into the coach and fell into his seat when the coach lurched ahead. Mei Lin caught him as he fell against her.

"You have nice walk?" she said.

"Yes. Almost got left behind." He turned to her, a mock serious look on his face. "Mei Lin, what would you have done if I had missed the train?"

"I find somebody travel with and buy me nice things." She smiled.

"Oh yeah, and where would you find this person?"

"Maybe him." She motioned with her head up the coach. Caleb looked and saw, across the aisle and five rows ahead, the man with the round, steel-rimmed glasses, sitting in a seat that faced the rear of the coach. He was middle-aged, dressed as a merchant of some sort, certainly not a man who made his living out of doors.

The man stared at Mei Lin. Caleb tried to ignore him, but each time he looked again at the man, he saw the same fixed, empty stare.

"Good luck," Caleb said. He smiled.

They rode in silence, looking through the window at the monotonous landscape flashing by beside the track, the distant mountains appearing to move by more slowly.

"I have never asked you about the Mad Hatter," Caleb said.

She looked still through the window. "There is nothing to say. You know about those places. Like Rat Trap. Same kind people. Same kind life. It make me sad to think about it, talk about it. Don't ask me, please." She turned and looked up at him, took his arm with both hands, leaned on his shoulder.

They rode in silence once more. Caleb closed his eyes, dozed.

Mei Lin stood and looked down at Caleb. She touched his arm. He opened his eyes and looked up.

"I need pee. Where I go?"

"Go up there at the end of this coach." He pointed ahead. "Just at the end, on the left side, there's a door. That's the toilet. If the door won't open, it's locked and somebody is inside. Just wait until they come out."

Mei Lin stood and walked up the aisle, bouncing about and unsteady at first, then easily down the center of the aisle as she found her balance.

Caleb stared through the window. He did not see the middle-aged man wearing the steel-rimmed glasses stand and follow Mei Lin.

Caleb drooped. He stared at his shoes. Each mile the train took them closer to Seattle, the sooner he would have to talk with Mei Lin. He rubbed his face with both hands, then massaged the lower back of his head where the throbbing had been increasing since boarding the train. His stomach churned, and he felt like his insides were being ripped out.

At the head of the coach, Mei Lin tried the toilet door, but it was locked. She looked ahead and saw the open space between the cars. Stepping up to the opening, she looked down at the coupling and below, the rocky roadbed and the rails flashing by. The rhythmic clickety-clack, clickety-clack of the steel wheels on the rails was louder in the opening, and she put her hands over her ears.

She turned when she heard the toilet door open. A woman stepped out, smiled, and held the door open for her. Mei Lin smiled and stepped in. She locked the door.

The man wearing the steel-rimmed glasses had stopped a few steps from the toilet. Now he stepped up and stood in the passageway, facing the toilet door. He leaned against the opposite wall.

The toilet door latch clicked, and he stepped across the aisle to stand before the door. The door opened, and Mei Lin looked wide-eyed in surprise at the man who stood there. He pushed her roughly back into the toilet and closed the door.

The man grabbed her wrist, twisting it. With the other hand, he tore at her dress top, popping two buttons open, and rubbed her breasts roughly. He bent, grabbed the hem of her dress, and jerked it up.

Mei Lin brought up a knee hard into his groin. His head came up, and his glasses went flying. Instinctively, he stooped to catch the glasses. She smashed the back of his head with a fist. He recoiled, released her wrist, and fell against the wall. She pushed him aside and opened the door in one motion, rushed outside, and the door closed with the swaying motion of the coach.

She walked quickly, ran a few steps, colliding against seat-backs on each side of the aisle. Passengers whose seats were bumped looked up and glared at her.

Caleb saw her disheveled hair and unbuttoned top. She collapsed on the seat beside him.

"Man, toilet, he feel me," she said, gasping.

Caleb stood and strode up the aisle, gripping seats on both sides, steadying himself. Reaching the end of the coach, he grabbed the toilet door handle and twisted.

The door opened. The man was on his knees, searching for the lens of his glasses. He looked up at Caleb, eyes wide open and unfocusing.

Caleb grabbed the man's coat, one hand gripping the folds of his sleeve and another his collar, lifted him, and pulled him roughly through the door and toward the opening between the coaches. He held the man's shoulders with both hands and pushed him into the opening and toward the side. The man looked at the flashing rails and roadbed below, jerked his head around to look wild-eyed at Caleb.

Caleb pushed him through the opening. Arms and legs flailing, he fell to the ground at the side of the track where he bounced and rolled down the slope and was lost to view.

Caleb braced himself on the coach doorway with a hand, breathing heavily, gasping, staring at the tracks flashing below. He wiped his mouth with a hand, flexed his neck, took a long breath and exhaled slowly, turned, and looked back down the coach aisle.

Nothing was amiss. No one saw. The man would not be

missed until someone at his destination still stood on the platform after the train had arrived and departed. Caleb hoped the man did not have children.

He walked slowly down the aisle. Reaching his seat, he sat down heavily beside Mei Lin. He did not look at her.

"I saw him. He dead?"

"No. I don't think so. The train had slowed on the curve. He'll have a few bruises to remind him, but he'll live. He'll have a long walk." Caleb put his arm around Mei Lin's shoulders.

"Are you okay?" he said. She nodded.

Maybe he'll live. Maybe I hope he'll live. He's probably a decent sort who just lost his senses for a moment. I knew a long time ago that Mei Lin would be a magnet for trouble. Not her fault. She's pretty, she's exotic, she seems so . . . so . . . out of this world. Out of her world.

CHAPTER 14
THIS ROOM HAVE NO COOK STOVE

Mei Lin stood behind Caleb at the check-in desk of the Panama Hotel, watching him signing the register. She held her bag in front of her with both hands and looked around the small lobby. Everything appeared new and gleaming.

The Japanese clerk, middle-aged, well groomed, and nattily dressed, looked around Caleb and smiled at Mei Lin. "I hope you both enjoy our new hotel. It opened just last summer. We are very proud of it, and we hope you enjoy your stay."

"I'm sure we will," said Caleb. "The key, please." The clerk tendered the key to Caleb, who nodded and accepted the key.

Caleb took Mei Lin's arm, and they walked down the hall toward their room. Each carried their bag. The clerk bent forward over the counter and watched them.

They stopped in front of their door. Caleb checked the key to verify that it matched the door number. He unlocked the door, pushed it open, and they went inside.

Mei Lin stopped in the center of the room and looked around. She still held her bag. "This nice, honee, but it have no cook stove, no sink. We stay here all winter?"

"No, uh, we're staying here only a few days. We'll go someplace else for the winter. You heard the clerk. We'll just enjoy ourselves here for a few days." He took her bag and put it beside his against the wall.

"It fine. I not be bore . . . bored! I . . . will . . . not . . . be . . . bored." She smiled, satisfied with herself.

Caleb took her cheeks in both hands. "Mei Lin. It's okay. Chinklish is okay."

"No. It is not okay. I want speak proper English so other people understand and so you be proud me. Proud . . . of . . . me!" She smiled.

He kissed her on the forehead and looked into her eyes a long moment. He walked to the front and looked down from the second-story window to the street below. She looked at his back, waiting. *Next he is going to say let's get coffee.*

"Let's go walk," he said, "get some coffee."

Caleb and Mei Lin strolled on the walkways along the water-front. They passed ships that were tied to the docks, American ships and ships from other nations. Crewmen lounged about the docks, smoking, laughing, speaking a multitude of languages.

They walked in Chinatown where all signs were in Chinese, and shops featured Chinese foods and goods. Mei Lin spoke to shopkeepers in Chinese, but she spoke hesitantly and said only what was necessary. On one occasion, she spoke English to a Chinese shopkeeper. The man frowned but nevertheless answered in English.

Caleb was surprised, but he understood. *This Chinatown holds too many memories for her, unpleasant memories that she would rather forget. Mei Lin, what is to become of you? And me?*

Walking in the middle of a narrow uphill street that was closed to all but local traffic, Mei Lin stopped. She held Caleb's arm and pulled him to a stop. He saw a puzzled look on her face.

"Honee," she said, "they are all men."

Caleb looked around. Sure enough, of the three dozen people in sight, on the street and in shops, only one was a woman. He had not noticed.

"Let's have tea," he said. "Do you see a teashop?"

She looked up the street. "There's one." She pointed to a shop about halfway to the top of the ascending street. They walked in that direction.

"You know about the prejudice against Chinese in Idaho," Caleb said. "It's like that all over the country. It's been that way a long time. Chinese came to this country because they heard that they could get rich. They planned to go home with buckets of gold, so they left their families in China."

Caleb and Mei Lin sat at a round table at the window of the small teashop. They sipped from small porcelain cups, looking occasionally through the windows, watching passersby. Hawkers, suited businessmen, the shop owner across the street arranging fruit in bins, a young woman with a little girl grasping her mother's sleeve, skipping and trying to keep up. They were all Chinese.

"But they didn't find buckets of gold," Caleb said. "When times got hard and Americans fell on hard times, they blamed the Chinese since they were willing to work hard for less pay. The same bad things that happened to Chinese in Idaho happened all over the west coast."

Mei Lin held her cup on the table with both hands and stared out the window.

"Then the American government thought they would solve the problem of hard times by saying that no more Chinese could come to the United States. The Chinese men who lived here couldn't afford to go home, and they couldn't bring their wives to this country, even if they could afford it."

Mei Lin looked at Caleb. "That very sad, honee."

"That's why there are Chinatowns in so many American cities. Chinese like to live among their own people, but they are also prevented from living anyplace else. They have to live in Chinatowns."

Mei Lin stared into her cup, her eyes glistening. "That very sad." She looked up at him. "But we don't have to live in Chinatown, do we? We can live anywhere we want to live. That good." She smiled.

He sipped from his cup and looked out the window to watch three old men in traditional Chinese dress walking slowly down the middle of the street, chatting and gesturing.

The light from the lamppost cast a soft glow through the street windows into their room, describing two rectangles of light, one on the floor at the foot of the bed and the other on the bed at their feet.

They lay side by side, looking at the ceiling, breathing deeply, Mei Lin smiling in the darkness, Caleb grim.

"That so good, honee." She turned on her side and snuggled on his chest. "Caleb," she said.

He turned over to face her. "Caleb?" he said.

"I practice, Caleb, honey."

He pulled her to him and held her tightly.

"Easy, Caleb, honey. Too tight."

He loosened his hold, with his arms still around her. He laid his cheek on her head, moved his hand down her back, her belly, and gently pressed her breast. He sighed heavily.

"Okay, honee?"

He was silent, then answered. "Okay." He squeezed her, then released her and turned over, facing the wall. He stared into the darkness.

The second-floor waterfront café overlooked the boardwalk and wharf. Ships were tied with long lines to wharf bollards, some loading, some unloading, others still and waiting. Pedestrians walked on the boardwalk, some in a hurry, knowing where they were going, others strolling, on a morning off or on a holiday.

Caleb and Mei Lin sat at a small table that overlooked the boardwalk and the bay. Their bags were pushed against the wall near their table. The entire wall where they sat was a series of windows from ceiling to tabletops. They looked at the bay where small steamer ferries and oceangoing ships sailed slowly by.

Mei Lin's plate was empty. Caleb had hardly touched his breakfast. He pushed the eggs and potatoes about his plate with his fork. Since they had sat down, he had hardly looked at Mei Lin, instead focusing on his plate and the bay.

"What is it, honee? You must tell me."

He hesitated, glanced briefly at her, then looked through the window at nothing. After a long moment, he turned back to her. He inhaled deeply.

"Mei Lin, you know that there are good people, and there are bad people. Many Americans like Chinese, but many do not. You know that in Idaho, there have been problems when Americans, mostly miners, have forced Chinese to leave their homes. Some Chinese have been killed. You know about all this."

Mei Lin's face fell, and she tensed.

"No, Caleb, honee."

"You know all this," he said. "It's not going to get any better. It's too dangerous for you in Idaho."

"No, Ca-leb, honee, please."

"I want only what's best for you, Mei Lin. I'm afraid for you. There's no life for you in Idaho, in this country."

"Please, Caleb, honee. I not afraid. I love you. If you want best for me, you let me stay with you. I love you. I do anything for you! I be servant, I work for you! I do anything for you!" Tears filled her eyes, blurring her vision. "I love you."

"Mei Lin, I feel like I'm dying inside, but there is no life for you here. You should be in China, among your own people, your parents and your family, your friends."

167

"I have no life in China. My mother father think I am dead. My life is here. With you."

Caleb stared blankly through the window, then back at her, then back to the window. *What am I doing? God, what am I doing?*

"There is your ship." He nodded toward the window. An oceanliner was tied to the dock below. She did not look. She slumped in her chair.

"I thought you love me," she said softly. Tears rolled down her cheeks.

"Mei Lin, I'm giving you enough money to buy a business. You are smart, you are a hard worker, and you will be a success in whatever you do. I know you will. You will be safe."

"You don't want me," she said softly. "You say you want best for me. Honee, China not my home. It is not."

He pursed his lips, said nothing. He stared through the window at the ship.

Someday she will acknowledge that this was best. I will be a shadow in her past, Idaho will be forgotten. As painful as this is now for her, and for me, she will heal and know that everything I did was for her.

She straightened. "You no love me. You throw me away." She wiped her face with both hands. "Okay."

She pushed her chair back, stood, and walked to her bag. Caleb jumped up and hurried to pick up the bag. She brushed his hand away, picked up the bag, and walked toward the door. He picked up his bag and followed.

They walked on the wharf alongside the large liner he had pointed out from the café. Aboard the ship, dozens of people, mostly Asian, leaned on the rail, looking down at the wharf, waving to those who had come to send them on their way. Some laughed and gestured, chatting happily with companions, off on a holiday. Others wore long faces, tearful, saying goodbye.

As they walked, Mei Lin stared at the wharf at her feet. Caleb watched her anxiously, wanting to talk, afraid to talk.

What can I say? What hasn't been said? What needs to be said? He walked beside her, watched her, wanting to speak, unable to speak.

They arrived at the foot of the gangway and stopped there. She looked up at him briefly, tear tracks marking her face, looked down at her bag. They stepped aside to let a couple, chatting and laughing, board. Mei Lin looked blankly at the ship.

Caleb held out a small purse. "Here is your ticket and money. Keep it with you at all times. Don't let it out of your sight. It is your future."

She took the purse, glanced at it blankly. She looked down at the tide that flowed slowly at the ship's waterline.

Caleb's face was distorted, in torment. "Mei Lin . . ." He reached for her, but she jerked her arm away. She looked up at him, and tears flowed.

She grabbed her bag, ran up the gangway, stumbling, her bag bumping into the side of the canvas-covered rail of the gangway. Caleb started to run after her, to help her, but she reached the top of the gangway and disappeared behind the line of passengers at the rail.

She was gone. Caleb stepped quickly to the right, trying to catch sight of her, and back again to the left, trying to find her among the passengers at the rail.

But she was gone.

At that moment, a dockworker at the base of the gangway released a clamp that held the ramp to the dock. A deckhand at the top of the gangway released a clamp, and the cable attached to the gangway tightened. The ramp lifted a few inches from the ship's deck.

"Mei Lin! Mei Lin!" Caleb ran back and forth, bumping and pushing aside others on the dock, trying to find her among the passengers lining the ship's rail. The people on the dock glared at Caleb, frowning at this rude fellow.

"Mei Lin!" Passengers aboard the ship looked down at the crazed man on the dock, shouting and waving his arms.

"Mei Lin! Come back! Mei Lin!"

Mei Lin's face appeared suddenly in the line of people at the rail. She pushed passengers aside to reach the rail.

"Come back!" he said.

She ran toward the gangway, then stopped, turned around, and disappeared into the crowd of passengers.

"My god! She's gone! She's gone!" he said.

She reappeared at once, holding up the purse. She ran to the gangway, stopped. The gangway had lifted a foot above the deck and pulled a couple of feet away from the ship's side.

Mei Lin leaped from the deck to the ramp, but she didn't make it. She landed on her stomach on the ramp, her legs dangling over the end. She slid slowly from the ramp, falling, her legs flailing.

Spectators on the wharf and at the ship's rail gasped. A woman at the rail screamed. Another shouted. "Help her!"

Mei Lin grabbed a metal rod at the end of the ramp with one hand and dangled. The ramp was now four feet above the level of the deck and was still moving away from the ship. She hung above water. Spectators gasped again as one. She hung by one hand, swinging, holding the purse in her other hand.

She threw the purse onto the gangway and grabbed the rod with both hands. She pulled up, straining, until her chest was on the ramp.

Then she slipped and slid off the ramp again, hanging with both hands gripping the ramp bar. Passengers and those on the dock gasped, screamed, called out for someone to help.

Crewmen had begun the slow process of lowering the gangway when they first saw Mei Lin leap for the lifting ramp. Now three crewmen at the opening in the rail where the gangway had been secured leaned out, trying to reach Mei Lin, but she was too far away.

Mei Lin pulled herself up inch by inch until she could grab the vertical poles of the side of the gangway.

Then Caleb was there. He had run up the ramp, bouncing on the sides, falling once, when he first saw her leap for the gangway. He kneeled and grasped her under her arms and pulled her gently to the bed of the ramp. She rose to her knees and picked up the purse.

Caleb helped her stand and supported her as they walked unsteadily down the lowering gangway, bouncing side to side against the railing.

When they reached the bottom, a crewman helped them step down off the swinging ramp onto the wharf. A loud cheer rose from the people on the wharf and lining the ship's rail. People nearby patted Caleb on the back and touched Mei Lin gently. Not a few people had tears streaming down their cheeks.

Caleb and Mei Lin held each other tightly. He whispered into her ear. "Mei Lin. I love you. I'll never let you go. Never. Whatever happens. I'll never let you go." She gripped his coat lapels with both hands and pulled him close, burying her face in the folds of the coat.

"Ready to go home?" he said.

"No."

He pulled back, frowning. "No?"

"I need to shop. I have no clothes. There my clothes." She pointed at the ship. The gangway was up, lines had been lifted from the wharf bollards and dropped into the water, and the ship was moving slowly away from the dock.

He smiled. "Little lady, we will go shopping. Anything you

want." He picked up his bag with one hand and took her arm with the other, moving her down the pier. People stepped aside, smiling, patting them on the back, wishing them good fortune.

They walked briskly, as if they had someplace to go. He looked up at the sky, then at her. "Mei Lin. Mei Lin. What was I thinking?" He stopped and enveloped her, pressing her head to his chest.

They walked again. "First, we need to get a place to winter," he said. "That will be home for a while. Then we'll shop."

She pulled away from his grasp and looked severely at him. "Okay, boss, whatever you say!" She laughed and grabbed his arm, ran down the boardwalk, pulling him along.

Caleb had not planned to spend the winter in Seattle, so he had made no arrangements beyond putting Mei Lin on the ship. He realized only now that his present and his future, in his mind, had reached an end with her leaving.

My god, what would I have done if she had left? What would have become of me if she had left? He shook his head. He didn't know. He had no idea. He had planned her departure, and he would stand on the dock and watch her ship leave. He felt a great sadness enveloping him.

"Honey, are you okay?" she said. She reached across the table and touched his hand. They sat at the same table at the window of the same small café overlooking the wharf where they had sat when he told her of his decision.

His head came up. "What a pair we are! Always having to ask each other if we are okay. Are we always so troubled?" He put his hand on hers. "Yes, I am okay, better than I deserve to be. Mei Lin, I have been so incredibly stupid, so wrong on so many counts. I am so sorry I did not listen, to you and to my own heart. I hope someday you will be able to forgive me."

She took his hand in both of hers. Tears rolled down her

cheeks. "Honey, I want go our room, and I want you to take off my clothes, and I will take off your clothes, and we will get into bed, and you will tell me how sorry you are, and I will say that it okay, and we will cry, and we will make love, and it will all be okay."

They stood, and he wiped her face with his hands. They kissed and walked toward the café door, with eyes only for each other, as if they were invisible, unseen by the dozen people sitting at tables, watching them, smiling and whispering to each other.

Outside, a cold wind blew the soft rain into their faces. They walked briskly up the hill, she put both arms around his waist and squeezed, and he leaned down to kiss her upturned face.

CHAPTER 15
I WANT TO GO HOME

With the help of the clerk at the Panama Hotel, the only person they knew in Seattle, Caleb found an apartment two blocks from the hotel. It was above a store owned by the clerk's aunt, in the center of Nihonmachi, Japantown. The apartment had a bedroom, a kitchen, and a small sitting room that looked out two front windows to the street. There were a toilet and sink, but no bathtub.

When Caleb questioned the clerk about bathing, he had shown them the metal tub that hung in the utility closet. But, he beamed, there is a wonderful alternative.

They walked to the Panama Hotel where the clerk showed them the sento in the basement.

The sento, a public bathhouse, had two gleaming marble basins, one for women and the other for men, filled with steaming hot water. He explained that patrons undressed and hung their clothes in numbered wooden lockers that lined the wall. The doors of the lockers were decorated with hand-painted signs that advertised local businesses.

Caleb asked the clerk where they undressed. The clerk was confused. Well, here, he said, as they stood before the lockers. What if there are others here? Caleb said. The clerk clearly did not understand the question, but he tried to explain. Patrons undressed before others, but they did not look at each other. They were to be invisible to each other. Oh, Caleb had said.

The clerk gave each of them a small towel to use as a body

cover, if they wished. Enough for Caleb, but not large enough to cover Mei Lin. The clerk showed them the faucets at the wall where they were to wash their bodies and rinse before entering the basin of hot water.

"Please remember," he had said, "never go into the bath with soap on your body."

The first time they went to the sento, it was afternoon, well before workers crowded the bath to soak their tired bodies, and it was almost empty. Only two older Japanese women were immersed up to their necks. The women had been talking and laughing softly when Caleb and Mei Lin came in, but now they were quiet and stared unashamedly at them.

Caleb opened a locker at the corner. Mei Lin faced the corner, her nose almost touching the wall, and began to remove her clothes. She handed each article to him without moving from her corner. She glanced over her shoulder toward the women, then turned back to her corner.

You poor woman. Every inch of your body has been seen by evil men, and every orifice of your body has been violated. And still you can blush. My poor sweet girl.

Caleb stood behind her, facing her, his back to the two women. When he reached into the locker to hang up his shirt, he glanced toward the women. They faced the opposite wall, but both heads were turned to look at them. The women made instant eye contact, but snapped their heads around and resumed chatting. Caleb smiled to himself.

"Honey," Mei Lin whispered, without taking her eyes from her corner. He bent forward to listen. "I glad there are no men. I don't like see men's bodies. They are ugly."

He smiled to himself. "Oh?"

She turned her head quickly to him. "I don't mean you, honey. You okay. Just other men. You know."

"Yes, I know." He kissed her cheek. She turned back to the

corner, removed her underpants, and handed them to him.

When they were completely naked, they sat on stools before the wall faucets and soaped their bodies.

"You want me to wash you?" Caleb said.

"No, women see. You can feel me in bath."

"Actually, I can't. I'll be in the men's bath, and you will be in the women's bath. With the two women." He looked at the women who faced away from them, chatting softly.

"Oh. Maybe you dry me after bath."

"I could do that, but I would have to face the corner." She laughed softly. He reached over and lightly touched the nipple of her small breast.

"No!" she whispered. "No do that!"

He smiled and took two wooden bowls from a shelf above the faucets, handing a bowl to her. They filled the bowls from the faucet and rinsed their bodies, then stood unsteadily on the wet floor. They replaced the bowls on the shelf and glanced toward the two women. They still faced the opposite wall.

Mei Lin and Caleb walked toward their respective baths. Caleb held his small towel over his crotch and watched Mei Lin. She held her towel at her waist in front, but her backside was completely exposed.

Caleb realized that he had never seen her naked body in daylight. Her exquisite naked body. He watched until she entered the basin. She nodded to the women, who smiled at her. She sank in the water to her chin and looked up at Caleb.

Caleb removed his towel and held it aside.

Mei Lin's eyes opened wide. She ducked underwater. Caleb smiled and stepped into the men's bath.

The weeks that followed were a cold, wet idyll. It rained most days, usually a gentle rain that was cold, but not unpleasant or restricting. They visited Chinatown where Mei Lin delighted in speaking to shopkeepers and vendors in Chinese. She bubbled and laughed, talking to anyone who would listen, all in Chinese. She held Caleb close, and they appeared as one as they walked down the center of the narrow pedestrian lane.

Passersby stopped and watched them. Mei Lin smiled and spoke to them. Sometimes she stopped and initiated conversation with other pedestrians. Caleb was content to stand aside and watch.

She had a particularly intent conversation with an elderly shopkeeper who stood in front of his herb shop, polishing a small urn as they talked. At one point, his jaw dropped, he looked abruptly at Caleb, back to Mei Lin, and he laughed until tears streamed down his cheeks. He looked at Caleb again, bowed sharply to him, and stepped into his shop, still polishing the jug, still laughing. Mei Lin walked over to Caleb.

"All right, what were you talking about?" Caleb said.

"You," she said. "They all very curious about you. This man, he asked if you own me. I tell him no, I own him!" She ducked her head, smiled.

Caleb looked at her a long moment. Then he bent down slowly, settled on both knees before her in the middle of the pedestrian street, and bowed his head.

Pedestrians stopped in their tracks, dumbstruck. They saw this American, kneeling before this young Chinese woman. They looked at each other, frowning.

Mei Lin bent over him. "Caleb!" she said softly. "What you do? Get up! You crazy!" She grasped the folds of his coat lapels and tried to pull him up.

He looked up at her, smiled. He jumped up, grabbed her around the waist, and lifted her off the ground. The circle of onlookers gasped, exclaimed, stepped toward Caleb and Mei Lin.

Caleb slowly lowered Mei Lin to the ground, took her cheeks

in both hands, and kissed her softly, hugged her tightly. She leaned back and kissed him.

The onlookers cheered, smiled, went on their way, chatting, looking back at the strange spectacle of an American man and a Chinese woman, deliriously and unashamedly in love.

They walked often along the waterfront, stopping at cafés for coffee and tea. Pike Place market was a favorite stop where they bought vegetables and fish for their kitchen.

On one occasion, they lingered over morning coffee in a small café, chatting softly, laughing. There were three other couples. Sitting at a window table, a Chinese girl held the hand of her white boyfriend across the table. They leaned toward each other so close that their noses almost touched. They talked softly, closely, closer, and it appeared that they would kiss at any moment.

Caleb motioned with his head toward the couple. Mei Lin turned and saw them. She smiled. It was not the first mixed couple they had seen in Seattle, but they always noticed. Quite a contrast to Idaho where they had seen no other mixed couple. What was unknown there was, if not commonplace, at least was not rare here.

They stood and pulled on coats. Caleb struggled with a twisted sleeve, and Mei Lin helped him straighten it. They looked again at the couple at the window. His hand was at her cheek. The girl laughed.

Caleb held the door for Mei Lin, and they walked outside, shivered in the sudden cold, pulling up collars and tightening scarves. They walked along the boardwalk, Mei Lin holding Caleb's arm with both hands, clutching him tightly against the cold breeze.

They stopped at a railing and looked out to the bay. Caleb pulled his hands from pockets and leaned on the rail. A ferry sailed northward, two small sailboats alongside, bobbing gently in the ferry's wake. Black smoke rose in a thick column from the ferry's single stack, swirled and scattered in the breeze. Passengers stood at the railing, looking down at the sailboats. A crewman on a sailboat waved.

Mei Lin looked up at Caleb. "You are quiet," she said.

He watched the ferry a long moment before speaking. "I thought I would never be happy again. I thought I would never be able to let the past go and live in the present. I'll always love her, Mei Lin, the memory of her. And Bobby and Sissie."

Mei Lin still held his arm tightly. "Honey, I never wanted you to forget. I can love them with you. I just want you to save a little place for me."

He turned to her and encircled her shoulders with his arms. "My sweet girl. You saved my life." He raised her chin and kissed her. "I've got a big place saved for you."

Mei Lin and Caleb, bareheaded and coats unbuttoned, walked in a small Japantown park. They strolled, going nowhere, their usual morning activity. Mei Lin's hands were pushed into coat pockets, head down.

Grass on the narrow park lawns was anemic and trampled. Planter beds were bare save for husks and dry stalks, some rose bushes that had not been pruned. Leafless tree branches reached out and up like bony skeletons.

The park gradually brightened as the cloud cover thinned and lifted. Mei Lin looked up at the sun through the dark, bare branches of a Japanese cherry tree. On the branches, she watched tiny droplets that had collected from the morning mist sparkle, drop, collect, and sparkle again. She stepped off the walk and stared intently at a low branch. Tiny, fat buds were just beginning to show a hint of pink. One bud, only one, had opened into a cluster of pink petals. She turned to Caleb who stood on the path, watching her.

"I want to go home," she said.

He stood a moment, then walked to her. "I do too, sweetheart. But it may be too early. There might still be snow. There's the pass at Galena."

"Could we get through?"

He pondered. "I could send a telegram to Ketchum."

"I have better idea. Let's take a train to Ketchum now and ask about pass there? If too much snow, we stay in Ketchum until the pass is open. How 'bout that?"

He frowned, pondered. "Hmm. That sounds like a good idea. Let's go to the station right now and ask when we can get tickets. Good idea, peanut! Let's go!" He took her arm and pulled and pushed her down the path toward the main street.

"Okay," she said. "Let's go!" They marched in step down the path. She stopped. "What do you mean, 'peanut'?"

"Nothing. Peanut, sweetie, sweetheart, love of my life, all the same."

She started walking, almost skipping. "Okay. I like 'sweetheart' best."

"Good," he said. They walked with long strides down the path, bouncing playfully against each other. He leaned toward her. "Peanut," he said.

She pulled away, hit him on the arm, and ran down the path, laughing.

CHAPTER 16
WELCOME HOME

Caleb stood on the wooden platform at the Ketchum station, talking with the railway agent, the same agent Caleb had worked with on his dredge hardware delivery. Bright sunshine contrasted with the piles of dirty snow along the roadways and perimeter of the station compound. Mei Lin sat on a bench at the end of the platform, her coat buttoned to the top and hands deep in pockets, her eyes closed and face turned up to the warming sun. Their two bags lay at her feet.

"The last wagons over the pass was four days ago," the agent said. "They had a time of it, still lots of snow at the top. Must not have been too bad, though. They turned around two days later and went back. Hadn't heard anything since then. I expect, I hope, they made it across okay."

"Hmm. I'm in no hurry," said Caleb. "We'll sit tight until another party comes over and gives us a report. Do you know where we can put up a few days?"

"You don't have much choice this time of year. Your best bet is the Idaho Hotel, just on the left side down the street here." He pointed. "Summers, some of the townspeople take in travelers, but not winter."

"Much obliged. You'll let me know if someone comes in from Stanley?"

"I'll do that," said the agent.

Caleb raised a hand in salute and walked to Mei Lin. He sat beside her. "Looks like we'll have to enjoy the delights of

181

Ketchum for a few days. Soon as somebody comes over the hill from Stanley to tell us about the conditions at the pass."

"How we go Stanley?" she said.

He stared at the empty tracks across the compound. "If we can find a wagon going over the hill that will take us, we'll do that. If not, we'll have to rent horses. I'd rather not do that since we'd have to pay for their keep until we can send 'em back.

"C'mon, let's get a hotel room," he said, "and then some coffee." He stood and reached to help her up. She batted his hand away and picked up her bag.

"Whatever you say, boss!"

He smiled, picked up his bag, wrapped his other arm around her neck and squeezed, and they stepped off the platform to the street.

The wagon rolled down the road above the cabin. Snow still blanketed much of the meadow, but there were dry patches that showed a hint of green. The sky was clear, but for a line of white, fleecy clouds. The snow-covered Sawtooth range was etched against a light blue background.

The pond was fringed with ice, but at this distance, most of the surface appeared to be open, sparkling, reflecting the drifting clouds. The dredge was tied to the shore where he had left it. Intact, from all appearances.

Caleb inhaled deeply, exhaled. He reached around Mei Lin's shoulders and pulled her close. She looked up at him, smiled.

"Look," Mei Lin said. She pointed toward the meadow. Buck and Chica stood like statues in the meadow just beyond the corral, ears erect, looking at the approaching wagon.

"Chica!" Mei Lin shouted. The horse lurched and galloped toward the wagon. Buck followed close behind. The two horses came up to the wagon and walked alongside.

"Chica, my sweet girl. I missed you." Chica bobbed her head, mane flying and tail swishing.

"Godamighty, Mei Lin. I never saw anybody who could hold a conversation with a dumb animal like you can," said Abel.

"Well," said Mei Lin, "that's because she's not dumb. She is smarter than a lot of people I know."

Abel laughed. "I won't argue with that."

Caleb had been relieved in Ketchum when the railroad agent had sent word to the Idaho Hotel that a wagon had arrived from Stanley. He was delighted that the teamsters were Abel Custer, the Stanley friend who operated the feed store, and his son Wally who had occasionally picked up funds at the Ketchum Western Union office for Caleb.

The return journey was faster than usual. The road was clear, the wagon was lightly loaded, and Wally was in a hurry to see his girlfriend. Abel refused his repeated request to drive because, he said, the young 'un tended to exercise the mules too much. He had dropped the boy in Stanley before driving to Caleb's place.

Abel pulled up in front of the cabin and looped the lines around the brake handle. He climbed down slowly, hopping in a circle beside the wagon to exercise stiff joints. Caleb jumped down and extended a hand to Mei Lin. She took his hand and climbed down. Both stretched. Caleb stamped the ground to revive cramped legs.

"Abel, you're a saint," Caleb said. "Thanks for the delivery. I owe you. I'm going to fire up the stove and make coffee. Can you stop a bit?"

"Thank 'ee, Caleb, but I'd best be on my way. Want to get back to Stanley before dark."

Caleb reached into the wagon bed for their bags and dropped them on the ground. They watched as Abel set the mules in

183

motion and turned back up the road. Abel waved over his shoulder.

Caleb and Mei Lin walked around to the side of the cabin. They were quiet, looking toward the pond and dredge.

Caleb cupped his hands around his mouth. "Halloo, the dredge!" he shouted. "Anybody there!"

Immediately two heads appeared from the door of the steam engine housing. Andrew and Cal stepped out onto the deck. They waved.

"Hey, Caleb!" Andrew shouted. "Hey, Mei Lin!"

Caleb waved. "I'll be down later!" The men waved, watched as Caleb and Mei Lin disappeared around the cabin.

Caleb stepped up the stoop to the cabin door. Mei Lin stood behind him. He lifted the latch and slowly pushed the door open. Caleb had warned Mei Lin that they would have a thorough cleaning to do before the place would be habitable. Spider webs and mouse droppings, an inch of dust and an assortment of bugs.

He saw instead a clean cabin, short lengths of wood stacked beside the stove, and clean windowpanes with an open curtain that admitted the bright sunshine.

Caleb turned to Mei Lin. "Welcome home, sweetheart."

The land was emerging from fire and ice. Tiny green shoots of new grass colored the meadow, still covered in a gray ash. Above the meadow, in the forest of black skeletons, some few trees that had somehow survived the fire showed leaf buds on the blackened limbs. On the forest floor, saplings pushed up through the mat of ash. Patches of dirty snow lingered in shady spots along the forest edge.

The dredge was back in full operation. Caleb and Mei Lin, Andrew and Cal, and Tindoor and two other Sheepeaters had worked dawn to dusk this past week to get it ready for the new season.

Everything appeared to be back to normal. Normal, meaning that they were taking little gold. Caleb hadn't sold any gold since putting the dredge back in operation these past two weeks, but he knew that they were not making expenses.

Nor had they ever made expenses from the dredge operation. He had always supplemented the gold income from his Virginia account, but he knew that this could not go on forever.

The first thing he had done on their arrival in Ketchum was to cable his agent. The agent's reply arrived just before their departure. The message confirmed that Caleb's account would be depleted by midsummer if he continued to withdraw at the rate of the previous year.

Caleb's back was against the wall. He had hoped to preserve for emergencies the purse that he had given Mei Lin, but he had begun dipping into that reserve to help meet costs.

And now this new problem.

A man stood in the cabin yard with Caleb, holding the reins of his horse, as Caleb read the sheet that the man had given him. The paper was a legal document issued by the County Clerk in Challis. The document declared that Caleb had not proven up on his claim. It gave him thirty days to respond and prove that his claim was showing a profit. If he could not do so, he must surrender his claim.

"I'm really sorry, Mr. Willis, the man said. "People in Stanley have told me that you're a good man and have worked real hard on your claim."

"I don't understand," said Caleb, "no one has talked with me about this. No one, so far as I know, has any idea about how much gold I'm taking. How did this begin? Where did this come from?"

The agent cleared his throat. He looked aside, then back at

Caleb. "Um, well, Mr. Willis, I'm just a clerk, but I hear things. My boss, the county clerk, gave me this paper the day after Mr. Bennett visited him last week. Now, I can't say for sure that there is any connection between Mr. Bennett's visit and this paper, but it's pretty well known hereabouts that Mr. Bennett does not look kindly on any dredging operation in the basin other than his own."

"Yes, I'm aware of that," said Caleb.

"Please don't say I said anything. I would lose my job, for sure. I just don't like to see a good man bamboozled."

"I appreciate it. Nobody will hear anything from me. I promise you that."

"Thank you, Mr. Willis," the agent said. "Good luck." He touched his hat, mounted, and galloped up the road.

"What will you do now, honey?"

Caleb turned to see Mei Lin standing in the doorway. "I don't know. I don't know how all this works. This is something new to me."

Caleb looked at the document, held it at arm's length. "Damn," he said. "Can I never have peace?" He walked to the door and sat down on the stoop. She sat down beside him. They looked outside, each in their own world, silent.

She turned to him. "I have a plan," she said. "I will go to dredge. I say to Bennett I want to work for him. Wash clothes, cook, clean. I get him into bed, and I cut his throat."

Caleb laughed.

"You think I can't do this? I Chink whore, 'member?" She smiled.

"Yes, I think you can do this. And I think you would do it. But I won't let you." He grabbed her around her shoulders and squeezed. She struggled, laughing and pushing him away. He tickled her and pulled her to him and held her tightly until she stopped struggling, and they faced each other, nose to nose.

"Why won't you let me?" she said softly. He held her face in his hands and kissed her lightly. He pulled back and looked into her eyes, brushed a strand of her hair with a hand.

"Because you're *my* Chink whore." He kissed her again. He stood and walked toward the corral, studying the document.

Mei Lin sat on the doorsill, her chin on her crossed arms over her knees, looking into the woods across the road.

CHAPTER 17
HOME IS WHERE YOU DECIDE IT IS

Caleb's wagon rolled down Stanley's main street. Mei Lin held the lines, and Caleb sat beside her. She pulled up in front of the general store and coiled the lines around the brake handle. Caleb jumped down while Mei Lin climbed down the other side.

They stepped up onto the boardwalk. Caleb spoke to Mei Lin and entered the store. Mei Lin looked into the dark interior of the store a moment, then turned back to the street.

It was a lovely spring day. Two old men sat on a bench in front of the feed store, adjacent to the general store, chatting, laughing, and occasionally leaning forward to spit to the street. Or toward the street since they usually didn't have the range, and their tobacco juice fell on the boardwalk.

Two women wearing ankle-length work dresses and bonnets stood on the walk on the opposite side of the road. They appeared to be talking, but Mei Lin could not hear them.

Mei Lin closed her eyes, smiling, contented, and raised her face to the warming sun. She opened her eyes and saw her.

In the middle of the street in front of her stood a Chinese woman, looking directly at her. The woman appeared to be in her sixties. Her lined face suggested a hard life, but it was a soft, open face. She was short, wearing a long black dress that would have been stylish ten years ago, with lacey white ruffles at the sleeve ends and a high collar, buttoned at the neck. Mei Lin glanced down at her own blue denim trousers and wrinkled calico shirt.

"Mei Lin." The woman said.

Mei Lin was startled. It was not a question, but a statement.

"Yes. I am Mei Lin."

"Nĭ bū rènshī wŏ, Mei Lin, dàn sī wŏ zhīdaò nĭ." You don't know me, Mei Lin, but I know about you. The woman walked to the boardwalk and stepped up beside Mei Lin.

"You are better known around here than you might think," the woman said. "People who are bored for conversation will talk about anything or anybody out of the ordinary. We are alike, you and I. We are curiosities. Wŏ mēn lĭang xīng yùn zhăo daò lē haŏ năn rēn, haŏ dē yăng gúi zī." Both of us were fortunate to find good men, good foreign devils. The woman smiled.

Mei Lin brightened. "Wŏ zhĭ daò. Nĭ sō Polly Bemis! Wŏ tīng shūo guò nĭ." I know. You are Polly Bemis! I have heard about you.

"Sī dē," yes, said Polly. "Mei Lin, wŏ mēn xīan zai yīng gāi shuūo yīng wĕn. Yăng gúi zī mēn bù xĭ huán wŏ mēn shūo zhōng wĕn yín wèi tā mēn bù dŏng. Tā mēn yĭ wéi wŏ mēn zaì shūo tā mēn." Mei Lin, we should speak English now. The foreign devils don't like us to speak in Chinese because they can't understand us. They think we are talking about them. She smiled.

"If what I heard is true," Polly said, "our stories are very similar. I also was sold by my parents and was brought to this country as a slave. I was taken to San Francisco and then to Warrens. The Chinese man who bought me operated the saloon there and expected me to entertain. It was a bad time for me. But the American who owned the saloon watched out for me. He liked me. Now he is my husband. I heard that the man who owns you is a good man."

"O, Polly, wŏ xĭ huān gēn nĭ shūo zhōng wĕn." Oh, Polly, I love to talk with you in Chinese. Mei Lin took Polly's hand.

"Wǒ zaì Stanley kuāi lǐang nǐan le cóng lǎi měi yoú gēn rèn hē rěn shūo gūo zhōng wěn. Kě sī haǒ dē, yīng wěn. Wǒ dǒng." I have been in Stanley almost two years and have never talked with anyone in Chinese here.

"But, okay, English. I understand." Mei Lin wiped a tear from her cheek with the back of her hand. "Polly, Caleb doesn't own me. He said that I am free and can go as I please. But I will not go away. I want to stay with him."

"Did you ever think of going home, back to China?" said Polly.

"No! Never! Caleb wanted to send me back, for my own good, he said, but I did not want to go. I refused. I said I would not go. I was very unhappy when he tried to send me back. My home is here. I think he wants me here now. He said he loves me. Did you ever want to go back?"

"At first. When I was so unhappy at Warrens. But when Charlie became my protector, and my lover, I knew my home was here. He also became my owner. He won me in a card game from my Chinese owner. But he said I was free and could leave if I wanted. I didn't want to leave. I wanted to stay with him. You see how alike we are."

Mei Lin motioned toward the bench in front of the general store, and they sat. They were quiet a moment, then Polly turned to Mei Lin.

"Mei Lin, home is where you decide it is, where you are happy, where you are with someone you want to spend your life with. We have been lucky, you and I. Most Chinese women who come to this country alone come to no good."

Polly withdrew her hand, and they sat in silence, looking at the street, looking into their shared, troubled pasts.

"I think I know how you got your name," said Mei Lin. "When I came to Rat Trap, men called me 'Polly.' But I would not reply. They asked me for my name, but I would not tell them. So they just called me 'whore' or 'Chink' or something like that."

"Men call any woman who works in a saloon 'Polly.' I don't know why. . . . You live on Stanley Creek? Your man operates a gold dredge?"

"Yes. But—nǐ bù něng gēn rèn hē rěn shūo—wǒ mēn měi zǎo daù duō saǒ jīn zī." You must not tell anyone—we are not getting much gold. "I don't know what is going to happen. He talks about farming or ranching or dredging some other place. I am worried."

"Mei Lin, you will find a place. This is good country. We left Warrens when the people there made all the Chinese leave. There were deaths. That was a sad time. Now we live on the Salmon, downstream from Stanley. We have a little farm, and we have good neighbors. Times are changing, Mei Lin. Americans around here are not so angry with Chinese as they have been."

Polly stood. "Now I must go. There is my husband." She waved to a man across the street who had just come out of the hardware store. Polly took Mei Lin's hand.

"We must be strong, Mei Lin," she said softly. "Baǒ zhōng nǐ zì jǐ hē nǐ dē haǒ yǎng gúi zī zhàng fū." Take care of yourself and your good foreign devil husband. Polly smiled, stepped down to the road, and walked across to her waiting husband.

Dawn, a clear blue sky. Tindoor and Caleb stood on the pond bank near the dredge. Tindoor and two other Sheepeaters had just arrived on foot, ready to work. Tindoor's companions had already boarded the dredge.

The dredge was in operation, and the noise was deafening. Caleb watched the bucketline chewing into the bank. At the other end of the dredge, a steady hail of stones clattered on top of the huge pile of tailings.

"Boss, I tell you something," Tindoor said loudly. "I said I would not say, but I must."

Caleb turned toward Tindoor and leaned forward. "What's that? I can't . . ." He started walking down the bank and beckoned Tindoor to follow. About thirty yards along the bank, he stopped.

"Now," Caleb said.

"Two hunters my village find two Americans in valley other side of village, a man and a woman. He hurt, shot. We bring to village. They say no tell anybody. I say okay, but he worse. Can you come?"

"Wait." Caleb strode back to the dredge, walked up the catwalk, and disappeared inside. A moment later, he retraced his steps to the bank and waved to Tindoor, pointing to the house.

Caleb, Mei Lin and Tindoor, riding one of Caleb's mules, rode into the Sheepeater village. They dismounted and handed the reins to a boy who led them away.

"They here," Tindoor said and walked toward his cabin. Caleb and Mei Lin followed. Tindoor opened the door and held it for them.

On the bed opposite the door, a man lay on his side. His upper body was bare but for a bandage wrapped around his chest. He was in his mid-twenties, drawn and pale.

He struggled to rise on an elbow, surprised. The woman who was seated in a chair beside the bed looked around. She was a few years younger, but the lines in her face revealed years of suffering.

"Tindoor," the man said, "you said—"

Mei Lin's hands went to her face. "Chica!" Mei Lin said. The woman looked up at her.

"Mei Lin?"

"Chica!" Mei Lin rushed to her, and Chica stood. They reached for each other and hugged tightly. "Chica! I thought I never see you again! Chica!" They separated, looked at each other, and hugged again.

"So this is Chica," Caleb said.

"Chica, this is Caleb. He took me from Rat Trap, same as you." She looked at the wounded man. "I remember you. You are . . . Ray!" He smiled.

"Yes. I think I know you too. Chica talks about you all the time. Mei Lin this, Mei Lin that. I'm glad to finally meet you." He extended an arm toward Caleb. "Caleb—" He grimaced in pain and withdrew the outstretched arm.

"Glad to meet you, Ray, and you, Chica. Now, let Mei Lin look at that wound. She's a regular healer, she is. She has doctored me, and she'll do the same for you."

Chica jumped up and held the back of the chair. "Here, Mei Lin, sit here." Mei Lin sat. She looked at the bandage, lifted it to see the edge of the wound.

"Chica, Tindoor, can you get me a piece of clean cloth and warm water?" The two went into the kitchen while Mei Lin began unwrapping the bloody bandage from Ray's chest.

"Who did this to you?" Caleb said.

"Polly's men. Two of them. Chica recognized one of them from the Rat Trap. We was working on the Wentworth ranch south of here, on the Boise road, and these two rode in one afternoon, saw me and Chica working on a fence, and started shooting. Just started shooting. Some of the other hands heard the shooting and chased 'em off, but they got me, and I didn't even know it till I fell on the ground. Good thing Chica was with me. But if they'd hurt her, I'd uh tore 'em apart, gut shot or no."

"I know what you mean," Caleb said.

"Why would Polly do that?" Mei Lin said. "She must know

she's not going to get Chica back. Or me."

Mei Lin still worked on removing the bandage. She stopped when the bandage stuck to the wound. "We'll wait for the warm water, Ray."

"Just meanness," said Chica. She and Tindoor had walked into the room from the kitchen. She gave Mei Lin a handful of cloth pieces.

"Water is warming on stove," said Tindoor. "Ready few minutes."

"Polly is crazy," Chica said. "She just wants to hurt anybody who goes against her. She's crazy. I don't think we will ever be safe, you and me, Mei Lin, until she is dead or gone."

Caleb frowned. "I think you may be right. How did you get here with the Sheepeaters?"

"I didn't want to cause problems for the ranch. They had only four cowboys other than the owner. I was afraid Polly's men would come back. Chica's right. Polly's just plain crazy. She just wants revenge."

Ray shifted on the bed, wincing in pain. "We left. I wasn't hurtin' too bad and thought we could make it to Boise without any trouble. But I was wrong. I was in pretty bad shape when Tindoor found us."

"We were hunting," Tindoor said. "Good elk country where we found them."

Ray lay in Caleb's bed, his chest wrapped in a clean bandage. Chica sat on the bed beside him. Caleb and Mei Lin sat at the table, holding mugs.

"I don't feel real good about this," said Ray.

"Just don't get too comfortable," said Caleb. "Soon as you're up to it, you're off to the bunkhouse. Mei Lin has already hung a quilt at one end, so you'll have your own apartment. Course, it won't prevent you hearing all the night noises from the boys at the other end."

"Or the night noises from our end," said Chica. "Sometimes Ray gets pretty noisy when we—"

"Okay, Chica," Ray said. "They ain't interested in our private goings-on."

"Oh. Yeah." She said. She ducked her head and smiled at Mei Lin.

Caleb and Mei Lin smiled at each other, sipped their tea. "Until then," Caleb said, "we'll be quite comfortable on the skins."

Mei Lin looked at the bed of skins and hides that Caleb had spread out at the end of the room. A warm feeling enveloped her as she remembered her introduction into Caleb's life, sleeping on her bed of skins, the comfortable, warm bed of her new life.

Mei Lin stood by the corral holding her horse's reins. She looked at the two horses in the meadow up the slope. The two mules grazed nearby.

"Chica!" she shouted. All four animals jerked upright, looking at Mei Lin. Mei Lin's horse broke into a full gallop toward her.

Chica walked around the corner of the house, wiping her hands on a dishcloth. "What?"

Mei Lin turned around and looked at her. "What?"

"Mei Lin. You called me," Chica said, "what do you want?"

"No," Mei Lin said, "I called Chica . . . my . . . mare."

Chica frowned. "You named your horse . . . 'Chica'?"

"Oh. Yes," Mei Lin said.

Chica frowned. "Why?"

"Because I love her," said Mei Lin.

Chica opened her mouth to speak, but she could not. She

closed her mouth, and tears streamed down her cheeks. She ran to Mei Lin, put her arms around her, and held her tightly.

Caleb stood under the pine where Mei Lin and he had taken their lunch so often. He looked at the jagged line of the Sawtooth range and the broad valley that lay at its foot. This country and this woman had saved his life. Now what was he going to do about it?

He lowered his head, studied the detritus at his feet, raised his head to look again at the mountains, and began to walk. Down the path through the lower meadow, away from the house, his head full.

CHAPTER 18
WHO DO I WORK FOR?

Caleb and three men were ranged around the cold stove at the back of the general store. They were in a spirited discussion, punctuated by an occasional friendly shout, a poke in the ribs, and laughter, then a stern face and furrowed brow.

The sheriff sat with Caleb on the bench in front of the general store. Caleb had made arrangements for the meeting to coincide with one of the sheriff's occasional rounds from his office in Challis. Caleb did most of the talking, the sheriff nodding often, pointing in Caleb's face once to make a point.

The deep green leaves of the arbor vines at Stow shaded the table and chairs where Caleb talked with four Chinese elders. The five sipped tea from delicate porcelain cups, the Chinese speaking softly, nodding often, listening more than talking.

Mrs. Ferncastle and Caleb sat in the parlor of the widow's house at the edge of Stanley. Her husband had died two years before, and her three grown children had scattered, one to Boise, a second to Salt Lake City, and the youngest to San Francisco.

She had served Caleb coffee and sugar cookies and now sat in a wicker chair across from Caleb's couch. As he talked, she frowned, then cocked her head, brightened and smiled, shook his hand with a firm grip when he got up to leave, nodded tight-lipped, hands on hips.

The small meeting hall contained five rows of benches on each side of a central aisle. All thirty seats were filled, and a few men stood in the aisles around the walls. The building was the largest gathering place in Stanley, except perhaps for the Rat Trap, and that was an interesting coincidence, for the Rat Trap was the subject of the gathering.

The building served as a schoolhouse for the valley's eighteen elementary school children, all that could find a means to attend since many lived a distance outside Stanley. It also served occasionally as a church house of whatever denomination that had a layman or itinerant minister who conducted services here. And it served as a gathering place for citizens who needed to discuss issues of interest to the populace. Like the Rat Trap.

Those in attendance included merchants, ranchers, farmers, and miners of all stripes. And four women whom most of those in attendance had rarely seen, the sporting ladies who entertained Rat Trap customers.

The four women sat quietly, huddled together on the last bench at the back, eyes darting about like small timid animals. Two of the women were well past their prime years in the servicing trade, which meant that they approached forty. The other two were newcomers, in their late teens or early twenties, already old hands in a profession that had a short apprenticeship.

Caleb stood at the front, facing the assembly. He looked down at Mei Lin, Ray, and Chica who sat on the front bench. Mei Lin, dressed in her Seattle finery, smiled at him and nodded. Andrew sat on the bench behind them.

"Thanks for coming, folks," said Caleb. He waited for the buzz of conversation to end. "I'm sorry that I wasn't more forthcoming about the subject of our gathering, but I had not finished with arrangements when I called the meeting. All I could say was that we would talk about the future and the part the Rat Trap will play in that future.

"Many, maybe most, of us have come to grief in some way by the Rat Trap. This saloon has been a festering sore as long as I have been in Stanley Basin. I'm sure many of you know that it has been a plague on the area far longer than that." A general buzz of agreement followed.

"This is going to change. The Rat Trap is going to disappear." People looked at their neighbors, and the buzz of conversation rose. Caleb held up his hand. "I have talked with a number of people who have agreed to take part in this transformation.

"Stanley doesn't need an abusive saloon. What it does need is a lodging house and a good café." The buzz erupted, including scattered laughter.

"A lodging house?" said a burly, suspendered oldster. "Who would stay there? Drifters and grizzly b'ars?" General laughter.

Caleb laughed, waited for the din to subside. "Folks, last fall, in Boise, I saw the future. I saw a motorcar. You've heard of them. I've seen one. They're coming to Idaho. It won't be many years before the roads between Boise and Stanley and from Ketchum to Stanley will be improved, and motorcars will carry people who want to visit the prettiest piece of country on God's green earth. They'll need someplace to stay." A few laughs, but most people were quiet, leaning forward, intrigued now.

"And they'll need someplace to eat. The main room of the Rat Trap will be converted into a café. It will be operated by two Chinese cooks who had a fine restaurant in Stow before the mill closed. They're sitting right back there. Lin Qingshan and Zhang Xinhu. Stand up, please." The two men, sitting in the back row, stood, smiled, and bowed. Scattered, restrained applause.

Caleb looked at Mei Lin, who nodded and smiled. His

pronunciation would do for a novice.

"The rooms upstairs will be fixed up as guest rooms. So travelers will have a place to stay as well as a place to eat." Nervous laughter and snickers.

A big man in the third row stood, squared his shoulders, and hitched up his trousers. "Who's gonna pay for all this? I hope you ain't thinking of passing the hat. It all sounds good to me, but I ain't prepared or able to pay for it." General murmuring.

"Good question. And I have a good answer. I've been in touch with my friend and agent in Virginia, and he's talked with a group who call themselves the National Union for Women's Rights. The group is concerned about anything that prevents women from enjoying political and economic equality with men. They want to help the women who are caught up in the Rat Trap web.

"They're right back there," he said, pointing to the back row. "Stand up, please, ladies," Caleb said.

The four women stood slowly, looking about timidly, appearing ready to bolt at the slightest provocation. The audience turned to look at them. Some of the townspeople smiled, but most were unsure how to react. A few people sitting in the front rows clapped politely.

"The Virginia group has agreed to finance the transformation of the Rat Trap from a hellhole to a community resource." Everyone turned sharply to the front. Loud, racous applause.

"One more thing," Caleb said. "Mrs. Ferncastle, would you stand?" Mrs. Ferncastle stood from her bench in the middle of the room. She smiled broadly, turning to greet the audience, front and back, enjoying the notoriety. Polite applause from the others who did not know why they were applauding. She looked at Caleb who smiled and nodded. She sat.

"You know that Mrs. Ferncastle lives at the edge of town on the Boise road. She is going to convert her house into a guesthouse for travelers and renters. The four ladies from Rat Trap are going to live in two of her bedrooms. And they are going to work at the new lodge.

"Mrs. Ferncastle's other two rooms will be let to travelers. She says she'll also serve breakfast to the travelers. She's going to call her place 'Sawtooths Bed & Breakfast.' Has a nice ring to it." General applause and laughter, a little back-slapping.

"What's gonna happen to Polly?" said a bewhiskered man at the back. "I don't suppose she thinks much of your plan, Caleb." General laughter and raucous comment.

"Yeah. Polly," said Caleb. "The sheriff gave her a choice. She can stay and fight. And get arrested for slavery, kidnapping, and attempted murder. Or she can take the cash that she has stashed somewhere, she's not dumb, and leave the state. And if she ever returns to Idaho, she'll be arrested." General applause.

"What option did she take?" said a man. Laughter and snickers.

"Anyone seen Polly lately?" Caleb said. "She left on a freight wagon three days ago for Ketchum where I understand she will take a train for parts unknown." Cheers all around.

"We're not sure who's going to run the place, but for now, Andrew, my foreman, has agreed to work with Matt, you know Matt, the bartender, he's staying on, to get things moving. Andrew may have to ride to Boise occasionally to talk with people who know about these things. There's Andrew," said Caleb, pointing to Andrew who raised his hand.

"By the way, Matt is keeping the bar open, but that's all the services offered in the Rat Trap at the moment. So let's adjourn to the bar and come up with a new name for the community lodge." Raucous cheers and back-slapping.

The people poured from the meetinghouse in a festive mood. The men headed straight for the Rat Trap, across the road and down half a dozen doors. Some of the women moved off to do neglected chores. Others tarried in front of the meetinghouse, chatting.

Mei Lin and Chica wanted nothing to do with the saloon, and they walked arm in arm toward the general store. When they were resident at the Rat Trap, they had rarely ventured outside. Now they were simply townspeople. This was the first time Chica had returned to Stanley since Ray had spirited her away.

Inside the saloon, Matt was singularly happy about the change in his employment. He busied himself, pouring from bottles whose ownership was uncertain, but this did not prevent him from filling glasses and ignoring the proffered coins from the men leaning on the bar.

One of the men at the bar turned toward his pard, spoke to him confidentially, but loud enough for half the population of Stanley to hear. "Davey, is this really Matt here, or is this somebody who looks a little like Matt? This ain't the Matt who's been pouring drinks here fer the two years I've been comin' to th' Trap."

Bennie nodded, leaned in, replying in like play-acting volume. "Yep, this is Matt. Born again." The two laughed and took generous swallows from their glasses. Loud guffaws from all who heard the exchange, including Matt.

"Everybody good?" Matt shouted over the din. A general chorus of approval followed. Matt took another glass and poured himself a shot. He banged hard on the bar top with his open hand. Everyone jumped as if shot and glared at Matt.

"I've got a toast to make," Matt said. "First one I ever did in th' Trap." It was the longest oration most had ever heard from him.

Matt raised his glass. "To Caleb! A damned fine fellow!"

The men raised their glasses and shouted: "To Caleb!"

"Hey, Caleb," said Matt, "who do I work for?"

"Everybody in this room," Caleb said. "But that's a good question." He turned to the room. "Before you boys get too drunk to think clearly, you need to elect a group of, say, five people, including Matt and at least one woman who knows this place better than anybody else in the town, to act for the owners."

"Caleb for president!" said a merchant who had consumed more than one glass of free whiskey and held his almost empty glass in the air. General chorus of approval.

"Thanks, boys, but not me," Caleb said. "I'm . . . too far out of town. Andrew can spend a night occasionally at the widow Ferncastle's establishment when he needs to do town business. But not me." He emptied his glass, waved to the room, and walked to the door.

Caleb and Ray sat on the bench in front of the bunkhouse. It was a cool, crisp morning and a clear blue sky that outlined the dark crags of the Sawtooths, and the warming sun felt good on their faces.

The dredge was quiet. The only sounds were birdsong and the rhythmic whomp up the hill of an ax striking dead wood.

"Getting along okay with the boys in the bunkhouse?" Caleb said.

"Yeah, everything's fine. They're good men, real easy to get on with."

"You're looking good," Caleb said. "How do you feel?"

"Good," Ray said. "Dying to get to work. I'm much obliged for the help and grub, Caleb, but this hanging around is gittin' to me. I need to get back to work."

"Where to?"

"I 'spect the ranch'll take me back. Soon's I can tell 'em that nobody's looking for us. Least, I think they will."

"I'd like to offer you work here, but . . . things are a bit uncertain."

"Thanks all the same, Caleb, but I'm a cowboy. Gold never held no attraction for me."

"Glad to hear it. Maybe we'll keep in touch," said Caleb. "See how it goes."

"I'd like that. Chica needs a woman friend. They're two of a kind."

"Same goes for Mei Lin. We'll keep in touch. Maybe . . . well, we'll see."

The lamp on the table cast shadows about the darkened cabin. Mei Lin sat at the end of the table in her chair while Caleb poured coffee into their cups. He returned the pot to the stove and sat on his keg.

They sat in silence, each sipping from their cup, staring at the lamp flame that flickered and danced.

"We need to get another chair," said Mei Lin.

"Mmm."

They sipped their coffee in silence. He stared at the flame, then at the wall, back to the flame.

"Okay, say it," she said.

He looked at her and smiled. "Now you're getting inside my head, peanut." She smiled. He leaned back on his barrel. "We're not making expenses, and prospects don't look good. My Virginia money is not going to take us through summer. We're mostly living on the purse that I gave you. We've got some decisions to make."

"I knew you were worried. But, honey, anything you decide to do is okay with me. As long as I am with you, it is okay."

"No, whatever we do from this point on, it's our decision, not mine."

She smiled, sipped her coffee.

"Then I can blame you if it doesn't work out," he said.

She reached over and hit him on his arm and gave him a soft slap.

"I'll still make some decisions," he said, "and I have decided that we need to go to bed. Right now."

She stood, leaned over, and kissed him. "Whatever you say, boss."

CHAPTER 19
A NEW COUNTRY AND A NEW LIFE

Caleb and Mei Lin held the reins of their horses. They stood in a copse on a hillside that overlooked the Pilgrim Fork. They could see the dredge, a quarter mile upstream.

Except no stream was visible. If there were a stream, it lay somewhere underneath the piles of stone tailings, fifty yards wide, that stretched like a huge bony diseased serpent from the barge pond down the valley where it disappeared around a bend.

"Honey, you be careful. I don't like this Bennett." When he did not reply, she wondered whether he had heard. "Honey—"

"Mei Lin, you were right." He stared at the tailings. "I haven't paid any attention to tailings before. They will always be here. The land will never recover. This must have been a pretty little valley once. Never again. It will always look just like this."

Mei Lin waited. She had never seen him so sad, so unsure.

"Mei Lin, what are we going to do? You should have gone to China when you had the chance. I have nothing to offer you. I have failed at everything I have ever done." His face clouded.

Mei Lin grasped his shoulders with both hands and pulled him around to face her. "I tell you what you are going to do, Caleb honey Willis. You are going to do what we came here to do. You are going to go tell Bennett that he needs to buy your dredge. We take the money and go away, start over. You failed everything? No. You took me from the Rat Trap, and you saved my life."

He smiled. "Yeah." He put his arms around her shoulders

and held her. "Yeah, I did do something right." He released her and walked to his horse.

"Okay, let's get this thing done." He stood beside Buck, staring at the saddle, pondering.

"You want me go with you?" she said.

"No, you stay. I don't think there will be a problem. Maybe I'll tell him that you are with the Sheepeaters, and you are all watching the dredge. Stay right here. I don't expect this will take long." He kissed her.

"I worry already," she said.

He mounted. "Don't worry. It's going to go fine. I'm coming back with a sack of cash." He wished he were as confident as his words suggested.

Caleb stood at the catwalk, staring at the dredge. It was deathly quiet. He reasoned that either somebody had died, or they were shut down for maintenance or gold recovery.

A worker inside the housing walked by the open doorway and saw him. The man stuck his head through the doorway to the outside to get a better look. He withdrew and disappeared inside.

Caleb waited.

Bennett stepped from the housing doorway onto the deck. He stared at Caleb a long, silent moment.

"Can we talk, Mr. Bennett?" Caleb said.

Bennett glared, hesitated. He stepped aside, leaving the doorway unobstructed.

Caleb walked down the catwalk. At the bottom, he hesitated, nodded to Bennett, and walked inside. Bennett looked up at the hillside, scanned the woods, and saw no one. He stepped inside the doorway.

Caleb and Bennett stood on the landing, overlooking the separating cylinder, now stationary, and the sluices below. All was still and quiet. The muffled conversation of two unseen workers below was punctuated by occasional laughter.

"What's on your mind, Willis?" Caleb turned back to Bennett. He had been looking below, listening to the separated, identifiable sounds in the absence of clanking and banging normal to dredge operation.

"I'll get straight to the point," Caleb said. "It's common knowledge that you don't look kindly on any dredging operation in the Stanley Basin. I've tried to understand why since I'm not in competition with you, but I'll let that pass."

Caleb paused, but Bennett remained close-mouthed.

"So I've got a proposition. I'll sell you my dredge and claim and promise that I will not begin another dredge operation anywhere in the Stanley Basin. Ever."

"Now why would I want to buy your dredge?" Bennett said. "You're not very talkative. Nobody's heard whether you're making any gold or not. I suspect you're not."

"Well, I can tell you this. I—"

"He's making gold, Mr. Bennett." Caleb and Bennett turned to see the man who stood at the top of the stairway that led down to the lower deck.

Caleb started. "You!" It was Cal. Bennett smiled, turned back to face Caleb.

"He's making gold," Cal said, "and he's found a rich vein since opening up this spring. It's got good prospects."

"If that's so, Willis," said Bennett, "why do you want to sell?"

Caleb glared at Cal, then turned to Bennett. "It's not to my liking. I'm a farmer and a cattleman. I figure that now that the operation is making money and has good prospects, I'll sell and make a fresh start someplace."

Bennett turned to Cal. "You prepared to run it for me?"

"Sure, I can do that. I know it pretty well." He grinned.

"Cal, you're a goddamned scoundrel!" Caleb said. Cal smiled. Bennett was enjoying the exchange enormously. He puffed up, smiling.

"Okay, Willis. You're willing to sell, and I'm willing to buy. At my price. I don't expect you're getting pestered by buyers."

"I haven't announced I'm selling. It's a going operation with good prospects. I'm not giving it away. And I'll need cash. I'm packing up and leaving the basin. You want to see my back, and you'll see it."

Caleb and Mei Lin rode on the well-traveled road alongside the tailings of Pilgrim Fork. They turned off the trail and rode into a dense stand of white pine. They ducked under low-hanging branches and through narrow passages between the trees.

Ahead they saw their wagon, the pair of mules in harness, standing quietly. A canvas tarp covered a heavy load, all they could wedge into the bed.

Cal sat his horse beside the wagon. He nodded to Caleb as he and Mei Lin pulled up beside him.

"I owe you, Cal," said Caleb, "and I won't forget it."

"No, you don't, boss." He grinned. "Most fun I've had in years." He sobered, looked down, looked up at Caleb. "I done you bad, boss, and I'm sorry. I didn't have my head on straight."

"It's all past and done with," said Caleb. "We were ready to move on, and I couldn't have pulled it off without your help."

All three dismounted. Caleb took the reins of Buck and Chica, walked them to the back of the wagon, and tied the reins to the tailgate.

"Where you bound?" said Caleb. "I don't suppose you're calling on the phantom brother in Bozeman."

Cal smiled, ducked his head, looked up. "Naw, that was Mr. Bennett's idea. Sounded kinda silly to me. Naw, I'm headed back to California. I got an honest-to-goodness big brother who has a nice spread near Grass Valley. He'll be glad to see me. I was a pretty good cowboy before the gold bug bit me. And nobody in Grass Valley will know Roderick Bennett."

"How're you fixed for a stake?" Caleb said.

"I'm okay. Payday was yesterday." He grinned. "Have to admit that I also dipped into the petty cash, going out the door." He laughed out loud.

He sobered. "How 'bout you? Where to?"

Caleb looked aside, up to the treetops, reluctant to take this last step, even verbally, this final break with a familiar past.

"Heading over to Wyoming. I hear there's some good cattle country in Jackson Hole for them that's not afraid of a little weather and a lot of hard work. Heard that the mountains look a lot like the Sawtooths. I like that."

"Sounds good," said Cal. He gathered his reins. "Well, I'd best make tracks." He looked aside, removed his hat, turned back to Caleb and Mei Lin.

"Good luck to the both of you. Boss, Miss Mei Lin. You're good folks." He stood beside his horse a moment, staring down at the stirrups, then turned back to Caleb and Mei Lin. "You saved my life out there on Stanley Creek, you know." He replaced his hat, mounted slowly, and walked his horse into the dark copse.

Caleb and Mei Lin watched him 'till he disappeared into the pines. Caleb turned to Mei Lin and took her in his arms. He pulled her to him and rested his cheek on her head.

"Ready, sweetheart? Now it's just you and me. A new country and a new life."

She leaned back, took Caleb's face in both hands, and kissed him. "A new country and a new life," she said. "We're ready, honey, both of us."

She took his hand and pressed it to her belly.

AFTERWORD

It is the careless novelist who thinks he can get away with making it all up. Being creative is one thing; doing violence with what is known is something else. I acknowledge my gratitude to a number of people who helped me get it right. If I failed, it is my fault, not theirs.

Thanks to Gary Gadwa, president of the Board of the Sawtooth Interpretive and Historical Association, which manages the Stanley Museum and Redfish Center. Gary was particularly helpful with answers to my questions about gold dredging in Stanley Basin. But he also instructed me on such minutia as native grasses and other plants of the basin, how locals made log cabins airtight and the chinking material used, the sort of stove they used and the type of steam engine employed on local gold dredges. He is the guru of all things Stanley Basin.

Allan Young, a mining engineer at the Bureau of Land Management office in Boise, advised me on the law concerning dredging claims in 1910.

I am grateful to Sherry Monahan who helped me put the right foods on the plates of my characters, and to Chris Enss who told me what they might be wearing.

Thanks to John Horst for many things, especially helping me find the right guns and accouterments for Caleb. More to the point, I thank him for his inspiration and his veiled admonitions to quit whining and write.

Anne Burke and Sue Eoff advised me on the appearance, performance, and care of horses, particularly advising Caleb as he showed Mei Lin how to take care of her mare.

I am grateful to the Pacific critique group for their careful reading of the manuscript and their useful suggestions.

Thanks to Sylvia Rambach and Charles Hwang for Chinese translation and names. The obscenities were my own concoction.

Finally, my thanks to Henry Willis for his courage in the opening years of the twentieth century to leave a promising engineering profession in the East to take up gold dredging in Idaho. I am grateful that he brought his family that included his youngest, Marion, who enjoyed her childhood divided between cultured Boise and the rough happy life in the cabin at the dredge site on Stanley Creek. I am particularly indebted to Henry for his decision later to settle in California's Bay Area where I met Marion's youngest daughter, my sweet wife, Carol.

ABOUT THE AUTHOR

Harlan Hague, Ph.D., is a native Texan who has lived in Japan and England. His travels have taken him to about eighty countries and dependencies and a circumnavigation of the globe. He is a prize-winning historian and novelist of the American West. History specialties are exploration and trails, California's Mexican era, American Indians, and the environment. His coauthored biography, *Thomas O. Larkin: A Life of Patriotism and Profit in Old California,* was awarded the Caroline Bancroft History Prize. Most of his novels are westerns with romance themes and, in one, a bit of science fiction. In addition to history, biography, and fiction, he has written travel and fantasy. He writes screenplays, including a screenplay based on *A Place for Mei Lin.* For more about what he has done and what he is doing, see his website at harlanhague.us. Hague lives in California.